A Quest for Dragons

Joab Stieglitz

Contents

Chapter 1: Srezzig's Awakening

Dawn cut sharp across the Fallen Scale Peaks, turning each ancient ridge into a jagged silhouette against the bruised sky. It traced the frost-covered crags in white fire, turned the eastern clouds brittle as glass, and threw long, amber shafts through the mist below. For a moment, the whole mountain went utterly still, as if waiting to be named.

Shyvnir crouched over the nest's edge, her massive body making the half-ruined fortress of broken stone and torn brush look like a child's abandoned toy. Her wings—veined with age and scarred from more battles than she could count—pressed tight against her sides. The bitter wind rattled her weathered bronze scales, catching on the old wounds across her shoulders and along her tail, where three spikes had long since snapped down to stumps.

Below her, the nest's center was a tangle of noise—tiny chirps and the scrape of newborn claws on stone. The last egg rocked in its hollow. Pale blue, its shell split with hairline cracks spreading across the top, leaking warm fluid onto the matted padding beneath. The other shells lay trampled and torn: gold, coal black, sickly pearl. Three shells, three hatchlings. But everyone—even the newborns—stared at the blue one now.

Shyvnir's eyes, gold and sharp as blades, fixed on the trembling egg. That gaze had once halted a charging wyvern mid-flight, but it couldn't crack this final shell.

She waited.

Ukshagg, the firstborn, edged sideways, watching the blue egg with a wary, calculating intensity. Her head tilted, nostrils flaring. Drozkax, all false courage and jittering energy, paced in a tight circle, eyes never leaving the blue. Hashaezkend, the pearl-colored runt, huddled near the nest's rim and whimpered softly, ribs stark beneath paper-thin skin.

Crack.

The sound was clean and sharp as a snapped twig. A wet blue claw punched through the end, slashed at open air, then withdrew. Nothing followed for three long, trembling breaths.

Then the shell burst apart. Membrane and bright fragments scattered everywhere, slick and dripping. The wyrmling tumbled free in a mess of fluids and hit the nest floor hard, legs scrambling for purchase. Shyvnir lunged forward, nearly flattening another hatchling in her rush to see.

Srezzig blinked against the cold, the sun, and the sudden agony of being alive. He coughed, throat seizing, and spat out a clot of yolk. The air tasted like metal and feathers and something older still.

His siblings formed a loose, uneven circle around him. The gold one, Ukshagg, watched with a cool, assessing curiosity. Drozkax, the black, coiled and hissed through stubby teeth. Near the edge, the pearl-white Hashaezkend trembled, unable to hide her bones or her fear.

Srezzig didn't care. Sunlight caught his blue scales, each one tiny but flawless, almost too clean for this world. His chest rose and fell in quick, shuddering bursts. His eyes opened fully: two rings of sea-glass green, wary yet unafraid, bright as a promise no one else could see.

Shyvnir made the only sound she allowed herself—a brief, dismissive grunt. Then her muzzle plunged down into the nest, smearing egg fluid across the bedding, forcing the blue wyrmling to move or be crushed beneath her weight. Srezzig moved. His claws scraped for purchase on the shredded straw. His legs worked in a jerky, graceless rhythm as he flexed, discovering new muscles, new pains, and the messy, bewildering work of learning to live.

The other three watched him like they expected him to drop dead any moment. Instead, Srezzig snapped his jaw at Drozkax, and the black wyrmling flinched back, bristling. Hashaezkend let out a noise halfway between a whimper and a sigh, trying—and failing—to curl into a defensive ball.

That was when Srezzig noticed movement at the nest's far edge. A fifth wyrmling, still half-trapped in its shell. The shell was paper-thin, nearly transparent. The creature inside had managed only a single small hole, through which it dragged desperate gulps of air. The membrane clung tight to its face, suffocating it by degrees.

Something pulled Srezzig forward—instinct, perhaps, or something deeper. His own birth had left him streaked with blue blood and egg slime, but his legs obeyed him now. With three awkward lunges he reached the fifth wyrmling. He clamped his jaw around the fragile shell's edge and pulled.

The thin shell tore like soaked parchment. Warm fluid splashed across his tongue. He spat it out and bit again. Hashaezkend shrank back, startled, but Srezzig kept tearing. Each bite widened the opening, carving a path toward freedom.

A nose pushed through. Then a trembling mouth. Then the whole head, bronze-sheened and dripping. Srezzig stepped back as the new wyrmling slumped into the daylight, gasped, and immediately coughed up the fluid clogging its lungs.

Shyvnir didn't move, but her tail lashed once—approval, sharp and unmistakable. Her breath rolled down over them in a heavy wave, stirring their damp scales and warming their fragile bodies.

Srezzig and the bronze hatchling locked eyes. Shrarzeth's gaze was unfocused but held something—gratitude, perhaps, or simple, primal relief. Srezzig hissed again, softer this time. Not a threat. An invitation. Shrarzeth croaked back, barely a sound. Her legs trembled, but she crawled toward Srezzig, drawn by the faint warmth he radiated.

Above them, Shyvnir's massive head descended, casting the entire nest into shadow. She inhaled, the force of it nearly knocking the hatchlings off their feet. Then her voice—deep, ancient, and edged with iron—filled the nest for the first time.

"Well. Only half dead, this lot. Could be worse."

The blue wyrmling, smallest and last, lifted his chin. It hurt, but he did it anyway. He didn't know what the world was yet, only that he wanted more of it.

He remembered the taste of eggshells, and the sharp, startling ache of being alive.

As the sun flooded the nest with harsh light, Srezzig's hatching shock dulled into a spreading ache. His goals were simple: don't die; hold your ground. He flinched as Ukshagg circled into his blind side, her golden scales throwing back cold flashes of dawn. Her movements were deliberate, calculated. She watched him the way a hunter watches prey, and when he snapped a warning, she merely blinked. He understood then: she wasn't afraid, and nothing in this world would ever make her so.

Drozkax, the black one, slithered along the nest's ragged edge, licking pieces of his own shell. His movements were twitchy and unpredictable—a wild lunge one second, rigid stillness the next. When Srezzig got too close, Drozkax puffed himself up with a possessive growl that was pure territorial instinct.

Srezzig ignored the meaning but accepted the message. He shifted closer to Shrarzeth, the fragile bronze who still hadn't figured out how to breathe without trembling. The little female kept trying to draw near the others, even though each attempt left her shakier than before. She edged up to Srezzig, brushed a trembling claw against his arm, and made a sound that was almost a song—soft, tuneless, but alive.

Drozkax saw the touch. His lip curled.

He slunk toward Shrarzeth, jaws open just wide enough to show the budding tips of teeth. Srezzig felt the black wyrmling's muscles coil, saw the strike forming. Instinct took hold. He shoved himself between them and caught a sharp scratch across his snout for it.

Shrarzeth squeaked and ducked behind him.

Drozkax kept coming, but Srezzig held his ground, sparks flickering faintly along his newborn blue scales. For a heartbeat, the world narrowed to three things: the black's hunger, the blue's refusal, and the bronze's helplessness. Srezzig's heart pounded hard in his chest, but he didn't yield an inch.

He stared Drozkax down, head low, jaw set, daring him to continue. Drozkax blinked first. He slunk to the far side of the nest and glared from a safe distance, sulking.

Above them, Shyvnir's nostrils flared. She exhaled a cloud of fog, then spoke:

"Squabbling is pointless. This world has teeth enough already."

Her tail whipped once, a single, punishing stroke that drove the lesson home.

Srezzig watched her—every shift, every angle, the way she held her neck high, how she made herself larger with nothing more than a tilt of the head or the slow flex of muscle. He wanted that. Needed to know how she did it. Needed to learn the shape of survival.

He tried to copy her. Chin up, spine straight, wings tucked tight. It was clumsy, overdone, almost ridiculous—but Srezzig didn't care. If posturing meant survival, then looking foolish was a price worth paying.

Hashaezkend, oblivious to the unspoken battle lines, hummed a soft tune that vibrated through the nest's battered floor. The notes rose and fell like small waves sloshing against stone. Shrarzeth pressed herself closer to Srezzig's side, her bronze scales still damp and shining faintly. Her breathing had finally evened out, though her eyes remained wide and painfully new. Srezzig draped a wing over her like a shield, the gesture instinctive.

Ukshagg kept her distance, head tilted, always watching.

Drozkax brooded in silence.

Eventually, the tension frayed into an uneasy truce. Srezzig and Shrarzeth huddled together beneath his wing, Hashaezkend humming in the background like a broken lullaby, while Ukshagg perched near the highest slope of the nest. Drozkax circled the perimeter, pacing and muttering, but he didn't go near the bronze again.

Shyvnir watched them all. Her eyes—sharp as gold blades—swept over each hatchling, weighing, measuring, judging. When Srezzig dared to lift his head and meet her stare, he held it. No kindness. No warmth. But maybe— just maybe—a flicker of respect.

Srezzig decided he'd earn more.

He crept to the edge of the nest, back arched, head high, pretending to stand guard. Maybe he truly was. The wind up here was vicious, cutting across his scales, but Srezzig welcomed it. Danger tasted better than helplessness.

Behind him, Hashaezkend kept singing to no one in particular, and somehow the quiet, wavering song made the ache of the new world a little easier to bear.

The morning dragged on until noon hit like a blade, and the air atop the Fallen Scale Peaks shifted from cold and sharp to downright hostile. The wind no longer simply blew—it came in vicious, unpredictable bursts that sent loose stones clattering over the cliff's edge and into the waiting void below.

Each gust threatened to empty the nest entirely, catching beneath the wyrmlings' still-wet wings and nearly hurling their scrawny bodies into the sky long before they were ready—tumbling them toward that endless, merciless blue stretching in every direction.

Srezzig couldn't stay still. Not with the horizon out there, promising so much more than this miserable pile of bones, mud, and half-rotted straw. His muscles twitched with leftover violence, but also with something new: the urge to move, to test the edges of his world, to push past them.

He started with his wings. The pain was old news by now, almost comforting in its familiarity. He peeled one away from his side, unfolding it as carefully as if he were defusing a bomb. The membrane caught the light between its blue veins, so thin it looked like a slice of captured sky.

He flapped.

It was pathetic—barely a puff of air. But he did it again. And again. Until the straw at his feet began to stir and twitch.

Drozkax, who had been sulking for the past hour, took this as a personal insult. He shoved his way to the center of the nest and flung his wings open with an overdramatic grunt. The membranes—oil-black and already torn in several places—caught the sunlight like a dirty, cracked window.

"Mine are biggest!" Drozkax snarled, whipping his tail for emphasis.

Ukshagg, ever the watcher, squinted at him and said flatly, "Actually, yours are shorter at the tips." She lifted two claws to demonstrate the precise difference, then nodded as though she had just presented an irrefutable conclusion.

Drozkax's jaw dropped. "Liar! Mine are biggest! Look!" He dug his claws into the earth, stretched his wings as far as they would go, and promptly almost toppled over backward.

Srezzig, already bored of the argument, settled it by stepping between them and flapping both wings directly into Drozkax's face. The black wyrmling toppled over with an indignant squeak. Ukshagg let out a sharp, birdlike giggle.

Hashaezkend stayed near the shadows, hesitant, her pearl scales looking dull under the shifting light. Srezzig walked over and nudged her gently with his nose.

"Try yours," he said quietly.

She did. Her wings unfolded like wrinkled fabric stretched too thin, each movement cautious, as though she expected the air itself to hurt her. She managed halfway before a cramp seized her shoulder, and she collapsed with a small gasp.

Srezzig propped her up with one leg. "Again."

This time, Hashaezkend managed to get her wings all the way open. Nothing elegant, nothing impressive, but enough to catch a thin slice of wind and actually hold it.

At the far edge of the nest, a small shape stirred—Shrarzeth, tiny compared to the rest, her bronze scales half-hidden in the shadows. She hugged her wings tight to her chest, shaking. Srezzig scooted over and tapped her side, persistent but gentle.

"Your turn."

Shrarzeth opened one wing, then the other, each stretch agonizingly slow. A shy little flutter followed—barely enough to disturb a single straw. She tried a second flap and froze, eyes wide with uncertainty.

Ukshagg chuckled. "Well done," she said, as if the words alone could make it true.

Drozkax snorted but spread his wings again anyway, and soon all five of them were flapping around in a clumsy, heartbreaking imitation of flight.

Dust rose. Feathers drifted. And the nest filled with something that almost felt like hope.

Above them, Shyvnir watched in absolute silence. Her wings, if she chose to open them, would have blotted out the sun. But she kept them folded, her presence alone crushing any reckless thought of misbehavior.

Finally, she spoke. "So much noise. You'd make better prey than predators."

Drozkax glared, offended, but Srezzig kept flapping. He believed—somehow—that if he could get this right, everything else would follow.

Ukshagg, meanwhile, had begun taking inventory. "Hashaezkend: fragile. Drozkax: strong but stupid. Srezzig: stubborn. Shrarzeth: scared. Me: flawless." She finished with a smug little grin that earned an immediate hiss from Drozkax.

Srezzig paused his practicing and decided it was time for something else. "Line up," he said, just loud enough to slice through the wind. The others stared, unsure whether this was a game, a challenge, or an order.

When no one moved, he said it again, louder. "Line up! Like this." He marched to the edge of the nest and planted himself there, mimicking the way Shyvnir surveyed the world—chin up, chest out, wings half-open.

Ukshagg moved first, intrigued by the notion of structure. Hashaezkend shuffled in next, doing her best to stand tall. Drozkax hesitated, but the competitive itch won; he shoved in beside Srezzig and headbutted him for position. Shrarzeth crept in last, wings wrapped around herself like makeshift armor, head bowed.

It was uneven, crooked, messy—but it was something. For a moment, the five of them stood in a ragged line facing the sunlit world. Each wore a different expression: Ukshagg's keen curiosity, Drozkax's barely-contained fury, Hashaezkend's trembling fear, Shrarzeth's fragile hope, Srezzig's stubborn certainty.

Shyvnir inhaled, and the whole world seemed to go still. Then she rose to her full, terrifying height, wings snapping open with a sound like thunder cracking over stone.

She leapt from her perch and landed in the nest with the force of a rockslide. The impact nearly knocked them all off their feet, but Srezzig dug his claws into the earth and stayed upright.

Shyvnir lowered her head until it hovered just above the line of hatchlings. "Show me," she rumbled.

Srezzig clenched his jaw and spread his wings as far as they would go. Ukshagg copied him, though her stance wavered. Drozkax, desperate to outdo them, stretched until his wing membranes tore and a thin line of blue blood seeped out. Hashaezkend tried, stumbled, and tried again. Shrarzeth opened hers just enough to make them tremble—a fragile flutter of effort.

Shyvnir's gaze lingered on Srezzig the longest. Then she showed them how it should look: a slow, deliberate stretch, every muscle flowing in sequence, a lesson in control and the shape of power. "Watch," she commanded, and demonstrated again.

They watched.

They copied.

They failed, and then tried again.

When it was over, Shyvnir curled her wings around all five of them, pulling them close against her warm body. The wind vanished. All that remained was the scent of scales and smoke, and the steady, ancient thump of her heartbeat.

Srezzig, tucked against her side, should have felt safe. Instead, he kept his head turned outward, eyes fixed on the world, wings twitching with wanting.

He was already planning the next flight.

Chapter 2: The Wyrmlings' First Flight

The sky above the Fallen Scale Peaks was tearing itself apart, molten gold ripping through the bruised black of the western slopes. The wind carried the sharp, metallic smell of snow and the sting of a fresh lightning strike. It whipped across the clutch nest, a crumbling shelf of stone and clay clinging to the edge of an impossible drop. Shattered obsidian and blue ice littered the floor, catching the dawn like broken glass. The entire structure tilted, as if the mountain itself were trying to shake them loose. There was no warmth here. No safety. Just height and empty air.

Inside, five wyrmlings were fighting to stay alive.

Shyvnir started the morning with a roar—not to speak, not to warn, but simply to make them move. Wake up. Get in line. Survive. The sound cracked across the dawn and bounced off every peak for miles. The echo alone could have broken a weaker brood.

"Edge. Now."

They obeyed. Srezzig went first, scrambling up the cracked wall with claws searching desperately for every hold. His blue scales looked almost black in the shade, his frame all angles and unfinished growth. Every step was a risk—one slip and the sky would take him.

Ukshagg followed, methodical and precise. She studied every foothold, every gust, watching how the wind curled around the rocks. Where Srezzig climbed like something driven by instinct alone, Ukshagg climbed like she was solving a complex equation.

Hashaezkend, the pale one, froze at the bottom. Her whole body trembled—hesitation, fear, the memory of falling—but Shrarzeth's silent expectation pushed her forward. Each movement looked like she was bargaining with herself. By the time she reached the top, her claws had left tiny, anxious scratches in the stone.

Drozkax barreled up next, stomping through the remains of breakfast—crushed bones, burnt feathers—without even glancing down. His wings flared wide as he climbed, as though he needed an audience just to exist. He shoved past Hashaezkend hard enough to make her squeal and curse beneath her breath.

And last came Shrarzeth. More compact than the rest, she already carried herself like their mother—rigid, focused, silent. She climbed without complaint, staying close to the wall for cover, but her eyes tracked everything, sharp and deliberate.

At the edge, the five wyrmlings lined up in a rough half-circle, facing the sun and the sheer drop beyond it. The wind hit them like a punch—cold, sharp, testing their balance and their nerve. Wings tucked tight, tails whipping for stability, eyes squeezed nearly shut against the spray of snow and grit that battered their faces.

Above them, Shyvnir stood like something carved out of bronze and time itself. She held her wings half-open, letting the morning light catch every scar and every ridge. When she moved, it was with a certainty so absolute it felt inevitable—no wasted motion, not a flicker of doubt.

"This," she said, "is how you live to see another sunrise."

She spread her wings.

The span was massive, the membranes thick and weathered, and the motion so smooth it displaced the air in a single rolling pressure, like a door closing on the world. For one breathtaking moment, the rising sun lit her up—a storm of molten metal against the breaking sky.

"Position," she snapped. "Hold."

Srezzig stepped forward first, far left. His wings were still half cartilage, barely formed, but he threw them open with a raw violence that dared the wind to break him. The membranes fluttered wildly, threatening to tear, but he braced against the stone and forced them to catch the air. His jaw clenched so hard it was like he was holding his whole body together with his teeth.

Ukshagg followed, slower but surer. She studied the angle of Shyvnir's wings, measured the tension in every tendon, and replicated it—almost perfectly. Where Srezzig was all instinct and nerve, Ukshagg was precision. Her wings held, though they trembled with every subtle correction the wind demanded.

Hashaezkend tried next. The effort showed in every trembling inch of her body. Her wings unfurled like overstretched silk, thin membranes rippling in the cold. She managed a decent spread, but then the wind bit into her joints and her muscles began to seize. She whimpered but refused to fold, her claws digging into stone for strength.

Drozkax laughed—loud and cruel. "Nice try, weakling."

Then he threw his own wings open—too fast, too hard—and the right one snagged on a jagged shard of rock. The membrane tore along the edge with a sickening rip. Blood welled up, dark and sticky, dripping onto the stone.

Drozkax didn't flinch. Not once. Instead, he bared his teeth at Hashaezkend and hissed, "Real dragons bleed."

Shrarzeth's eyes flicked from her mother to her siblings, dismissing their varied failures in a single, sweeping gaze. When her turn came, she positioned her wings not in imitation, but with an unnerving, innate understanding of their mother's form. Not the strongest, not the loudest— but unmistakably the most observant.

The wind screamed across the ledge. The nest shuddered under their feet. All five struggled to hold the pose, small muscles burning with effort.

Shyvnir moved down the line, inspecting each one in turn. She nudged Srezzig's elbow into a better angle. Twisted Ukshagg's wrist until her wing caught the wind properly. She crouched beside Hashaezkend and murmured, "Steady," in a voice that—just for a heartbeat—wasn't cruel. For Drozkax, she offered nothing but a dismissive snort.

When she reached Shrarzeth, she paused. The two locked eyes, and for a moment, the whole world narrowed to their shared breath. Then the matron nodded once—small, simple, significant—and moved on.

For three long minutes—an eternity for untested bodies—the clutch held. The wind tore at them, nearly knocking the smallest backward and actually wrenching Drozkax's injured wing out of position once. But Shyvnir's presence, that relentless, merciless stare, kept them upright.

At last, Shyvnir snapped her wings shut. The sound cracked like thunder ripping stone.

"Good enough," she said. "For hatchlings."

Srezzig dropped first, collapsing against the wall and gasping for breath. Ukshagg folded her wings in perfect reverse order, muttering equations to herself. Hashaezkend managed a controlled fall, cradling her fragile membranes like they might shatter. Drozkax wobbled, blood still dripping from the torn edge of his wing, but shot Srezzig a look filled with undiluted hatred.

Shrarzeth was the last to move. She stayed upright, wings still open, eyes fixed on the horizon. When the sun hit her back, her silhouette sharpened— a smaller, fiercer echo of the matron herself.

The lesson was done, but the day had barely begun.

At the edge, the nest trembled in the rising wind, and five wyrmlings stared at the empty sky—some with fear, some with hunger, but all with the bone-deep understanding that, for now, they had survived.

At the edge of the world, flight began with falling.

Srezzig went first—blue-scaled, bruised, and already aching from every lesson that came before. The matron's words still rang in his skull as he stretched his wings wide, tensed every sore tendon, and hurled himself off the ledge.

For one heartbeat, it worked. The wind caught him, lifted his foreclaws clean off the nest. For another heartbeat, he hovered there—uncertain, suspended by nothing but raw instinct and sheer nerve.

Then gravity remembered him.

Srezzig plummeted. He slammed belly-first onto the ledge below, claws ripping through lichen and dried scat. He skidded forward, bashed his snout on a jagged rock, and stopped just shy of a crack deep enough to end him.

It hurt like hell—but not enough to stop him. Srezzig shook it off, stretched his wings again, and began climbing back toward the nest. Above him, four wyrmlings stared down, wide-eyed with some strange blend of awe and terror.

Ukshagg watched from the highest boulder, her gaze flicking between Srezzig and the shifting wind currents along the ridge. She looked utterly stumped, like a hatchling facing a puzzle carved out of sky—but her tail twitched with steady, measured thought.

Hashaezkend stood frozen at the rim, staring straight down at Srezzig's crumpled landing. She wanted to jump—he could see that—but the fear of ending up like him kept her claws locked onto the stone.

Drozkax wasn't feeling generous. "What's the matter, princess? Scared you'll ruin those pretty little wings?" His laugh cut through the wind, harsh and slicing.

Hashaezkend flinched, drawing her limbs tight. But the sky called to her anyway. She took a trembling breath, crept forward, and spread her wings—delicate, gleaming, heartbreakingly fragile.

She jumped.

For a moment, it was beautiful. Light caught her pale wings and shattered into broken rainbows. Her small body arced gracefully, gliding two full lengths before the wind struck her side.

It flipped her completely.

She tumbled through the air, screaming—a thin, clear sound that bounced off the granite cliffs. Srezzig, still climbing, lurched sideways and braced himself.

Hashaezkend crashed into him. They both went tumbling in a chaotic tangle of wings and panic. The nest above shrank. The rocks below rushed up.

Srezzig swallowed his terror whole. He lunged, catching her wing-joint with his foreclaws and sinking the talons of his free foot into a fissure of rock. The jolt nearly tore his wing from its socket, but it stopped their fall.

They hung there, gasping. For a moment, simply being alive felt like victory.

Above them, Drozkax doubled over laughing. "Real graceful," he wheezed, then strutted to the edge and flexed every muscle like he was performing for an audience.

Ukshagg kept muttering to herself. "The updrafts are stronger on the eastern face. If you angle your wings to increase surface area—"

"Shut it," Drozkax snapped. "Watch and learn."

He didn't hesitate. He just jumped.

His wings snapped open with a crack, caught the wind, and for three glorious body lengths he looked magnificent—strong, steady, almost regal.

Then the wind shifted.

He overcorrected, stalled, and dropped like a stone. He scraped against the cliffside, clawed at empty air, and screamed all the way down.

He hit hard enough to knock the wind out of him and wipe the smugness clean off his face. But Drozkax scrambled upright anyway, glared at the cliff like it had personally betrayed him, and yelled, "Did you see how far I made it?"

Ukshagg nodded slowly. "Good start, but you lost lift at the—"

"Don't care," Drozkax snapped, cutting her off. "I did better than blue boy."

Srezzig—halfway up the cliff with Hashaezkend still clinging to his back—spat blood onto the rock. "You crashed," he growled. "Same as everyone else."

Ukshagg ignored them both. She kept watching—the wind, the clouds, the subtle way her feathers ruffled along her forearm. "Wait for the next gust," she murmured. "It's stronger. More consistent."

From the shadows near the rim, Shrarzeth stepped forward—silent, steady, unshaken. Her bronze scales caught the light; her eyes tracked every fall, every small victory, every twitch of air. Without a word, she spread her wings.

Everyone stopped to watch.

She lifted off in one smooth motion. Rode the wind without hesitation—no fumbling, no panic, wings locked at exactly the right angle. She glided past all of them, sailed two full nest-widths down the mountain, and landed without a sound.

Nobody spoke.

Drozkax scoffed, but didn't move. Ukshagg's tail twitched with something dangerously close to respect. Hashaezkend could only gape. Srezzig blinked, stunned.

Then—as if her success had challenged the sky itself—they tried again.

Srezzig climbed.

Hashaezkend followed, jumping only when Srezzig shoved her at exactly the right moment.

Drozkax threw himself off the ledge with wild, angry determination.

Ukshagg waited, eyes half-lidded, counting the wind's rhythm before she finally leapt.

Each attempt carried them a little farther. The cliff face became a map of their efforts—streaks of blue blood, shredded feathers, and scraped stone marking every mistake.

For an hour, the nest dissolved into chaos—battered scales, torn wings, shaking limbs, bruised pride. The air smelled like sweat and blood and the particular staleness of a space that had been closed up too long—but underneath it, something else. The smell of a room where windows were about to be opened.

Shyvnir, the matron, watched it all without a sound. Finally, when their strength was gone and none of them could climb another inch, she spoke.

"Failure is the only teacher that never lies."

Her voice carried across the peaks like a verdict.

At the rim, five wyrmlings huddled together—Srezzig, Hashaezkend, Drozkax, Ukshagg, and Shrarzeth—waiting for whatever came next. Above them, the sky stretched wide and merciless and, suddenly, almost possible.

The nest wouldn't let them rest. Barely a moment after they collapsed, gasping for breath, the wind picked up again—sharper now, colder, carrying the bite of fresh snow and the heavy scent of a storm rolling in. The world wanted more from them.

Shyvnir didn't bother with orders this time. She simply walked to the edge, each step deliberate and heavy with purpose, and looked down at her children below. Then she spread her wings and jumped.

No buildup. No warning. Just pure, blinding motion.

She swept out over the chasm in a single explosive burst, wings slicing the air like honed blades. In the rising morning light, her shadow stretched across the opposite cliff—a fleeting glimpse of what the hatchlings might one day become, if they survived long enough to try.

She hung there for an impossible heartbeat, utterly still, then spiraled downward in one long, elegant descent, every feather perfectly aligned. When she landed, the impact cracked a boulder beneath her claws.

The message could not have been clearer: *this is the goal. Nothing less.*

Srezzig felt the lesson hit like a physical blow. His body was screaming, every muscle raw and begging for rest, but the pull to rise again was stronger. He turned to the others, voice ragged but commanding.

"Again. Together this time."

Ukshagg nodded, surprise flickering across her face before she buried it beneath calculation. "There's a gap in the wind pattern. Twelve heartbeats from now. That's when we jump."

Srezzig didn't argue. He dug his claws into the nest's edge and began counting.

"Three, two, one—go."

Hashaezkend, carried by Srezzig's determination, didn't hesitate. Her pearl wings were battered and trembled at the edges, but they found a shaky rhythm in the chaos.

Drozkax, still bleeding from earlier, snarled and hurled himself forward, desperate to outdo them all.

Shrarzeth watched their mother one more time, copied her stance perfectly, and leapt last.

Five wyrmlings—nothing but instinct, wild hope, and stubborn will—launched themselves into the open air.

The updraft slammed into them. For one impossible second, they were truly flying.

Their wings beat together—a storm of blue, gold, pearl, black, and bronze. The force of their lift sent dust and loose feathers spiraling upward around them.

Everything slowed. The wind roared, but for that one moment, they rode it. Each wyrmling held frozen in the air: Srezzig at the front, jaws locked in a silent, desperate roar; Hashaezkend close behind, eyes bright with disbelief; Ukshagg perfectly aligned, caught between calculation and awe; Drozkax barely controlled, muscles straining for more height; and Shrarzeth, mirroring their mother exactly, wings arched at the perfect angle.

Then it fell apart.

The wind shifted.

Srezzig lost it first, tumbling sideways into Drozkax, who immediately latched on with teeth and claws. Hashaezkend, the lightest of them all, was caught in a crosswind and spun away, shrieking—half terrified, half exhilarated. Ukshagg saw the change coming and tried to correct, but the same gust that struck Srezzig slammed into Shrarzeth from below, throwing her uncontrollably into Ukshagg's path.

They crashed. Hard. A chaotic tangle of limbs, wings, and shouted curses, slamming into the nest and rolling until they collapsed in a bruised, breathless heap.

For a moment, nobody moved.

Then Drozkax—pinned under Srezzig and half-smothered by Hashaezkend's wing—started laughing. The sound scraped out of him, rough and cracked, equal parts pain and triumph.

"Did you *see* that?" he wheezed. "We actually flew."

Ukshagg, battered but grinning through the ache, corrected him with clinical satisfaction. "Six seconds. But yes. We flew."

Hashaezkend, still dazed, tilted her face toward the sky. For the first time, she didn't flinch. Didn't shrink. She simply breathed.

Srezzig said nothing. He lay there with his wings splayed wide, chest heaving, clinging to the memory of what the sky had felt like—light, wild, impossible.

Above them, Shyvnir watched. Silent. Still.

She stood there long enough for the wind to shift twice and the shadows to crawl across the stone. Then she gave the smallest nod—so slight it could have been a trick of the light—and turned away.

It was all the approval they would ever get.

Shrarzeth moved quietly between them. She pressed her scales against Hashaezkend's swollen wing, and where she touched, the vibrant bronze of her own hide seemed to dim, leaching into the healing. She soothed the raw edges of Drozkax's side with her tongue, each stroke leaving her looking more drained.

When she reached Srezzig, her scales were the color of dull clay. She lowered her head and breathed a soft mist across his shoulder. The cold numbness sank deep, easing the worst of the ache. The pain faded—but the lesson, and the cost, stayed.

Next time, he told himself, he'd last seven seconds. Maybe longer.

The sun climbed higher, burning away the last scraps of frost clinging to the stones. Below them, the world stretched out—vast, merciless, patient.

Waiting.

The clutch would be ready.

Chapter 3: The Blink Ram Challenge

Five mornings had passed since Shyvnir's ultimatum, and each had arrived worse than the one before. But today's light didn't simply creep across the Fallen Scale Peaks—it struck them. It hammered the ridges, shoved the darkness into the ravines, and set the eastern sky ablaze. The clutch cave shuddered beneath the crosswind, every loose stone rattling like dice in a cup. After nearly a week of relentless preparation, the moment had finally arrived.

Shyvnir summoned her brood.

Five wyrmlings clung to the crumbling lip of the nest, gathered in a ragged arc above the dizzying drop. The nest had never been comfortable, but now it looked ready to disintegrate if someone so much as breathed wrong. The last freeze had shifted the boulders again, skewing the whole structure sideways. It wouldn't last another season.

Neither would they—unless they learned.

Shyvnir perched atop a broken spire overlooking the nest, wings half-spread against the wind. Morning light washed over her bronze scales, each one etched with old silver scars, casting fractured reflections across the stone. Her ancient eyes narrowed as she studied her clutch, jaw locked in the hard, unforgiving line that had sent countless wyrmlings to their first, and often final, test.

"All of you. Forward."

She didn't raise her voice. She never needed to. The command hit them like falling stones.

Srezzig moved first, his stride deliberately paced to show no weakness. His blue scales gleamed with health, but he held his left shoulder—still raw from yesterday's crash—unnaturally still. He ignored the sting and met the matron's gaze without blinking, challenging her to find fault.

Drozkax stalked up beside him, black scales glinting as he crouched low, tail lashing behind him. His right wing still bled from a fresh tear, and he hadn't bothered to favor it. He planted his claws wide, bared every tooth, and grinned like he expected a fight.

Ukshagg approached by watching the wind ripple across the stones before taking each step, adjusting her pace to the shifting currents. Her golden scales had a muted, metallic gleam, as though polished into shape rather than grown. She stopped at an exact distance—close enough to hear every word, far enough to retreat if needed.

Hashaezkend and Shrarzeth lingered behind them, pearl and bronze swallowed by the morning glare. The pearl-colored wyrmling seemed to fold inward, wings pressed tight, trembling with each breath. Shrarzeth looked up at the matron, then mirrored the way Shyvnir spread her claws for balance. She moved forward with small, deliberate steps—wobbling, but upright.

Shyvnir let the silence press down, a physical weight that made each wyrmling feel her judgment. Her voice, when it came, didn't break the tension but sharpened it to a blade's edge.

"Today is your first cull. You will descend the slopes, cross the ravine, and bring back blink rams. No food until you succeed. No assistance if you fail." Her tail cracked against the rock, scattering stone splinters across the ledge. "If you return empty, don't return at all."

The words didn't echo. They didn't need to.

Her gaze slid to Srezzig first.

"You. Blue. You lead. Show the others how to land a blow that doesn't shame me."

Srezzig's spines bristled. He dipped his head in a slow, deliberate nod, then tilted it just enough to imply that leading had never been in question. "I'll return first," he said. "And I'll take the best ram."

"Only if you make it," the matron replied. "Last time you nearly gutted yourself on a boulder."

Srezzig flicked a claw, unimpressed.

Drozkax's hackles rose. "I'll do it. My wings are stronger than his," he snapped, locking eyes with Srezzig like a challenge. "We'll see who brings back more meat."

Shyvnir fixed him with a stare sharp enough to strip away every shred of swagger. "Bring back two, then. Or don't come back."

Drozkax grinned, but his neck frill had gone flat.

Ukshagg—still tracing routes in the scree with one methodical talon—spoke without lifting her gaze. "If we cut along the leeward side, we avoid the worst winds and the avalanche debris. Blink rams won't spot us through the shadows." She paused, calculating. "But the climb's twice as long."

Shyvnir's eyes narrowed, a rare flicker of approval. "Your way may be slower, but you'll eat better. If you survive."

Ukshagg nodded to herself as though she'd already mapped every risk.

Then Shyvnir turned on Hashaezkend. The pearl-colored wyrmling's wings trembled in the cold. The matron leaned in until her breath—thick with the scent of blood, raw fish, and morning frost—washed over the hatchling's head. "You will not slow them down. If you collapse, the others leave you."

Hashaezkend's reply trembled but didn't break. "Understood." Her eyes stayed down, yet her jaw locked with grim resolve.

Shyvnir stepped back and eyed the smallest. "And you, little one?"

Shrarzeth squared her stance, mirroring Shyvnir with startling accuracy. "I'll bring back the biggest one," she declared. "I'll eat its eyes first."

The fierceness of it made even Drozkax blink.

Shyvnir didn't smile. She didn't need to.

Her voice dropped to a tone older than the stone beneath them—low, heavy, unyielding. "This hunt will test everything you've learned. "The slopes will not kill you with cold or hunger if something else finds you first." Stay together until the kill. After that, only the strongest return."

She let the words settle, heavy as froststone.

"Go."

No further instruction. No warning. Shyvnir kicked off the spire, wings detonating the stillness, and vanished into the white glare of morning. The wind howled in her absence, raw and merciless, and with the matron gone there was nothing left to break its fury.

Srezzig immediately shoved his way to the edge, scanning for the cleanest descent. The path below was chaos—loose shale, broken stone, and jutting blades of rock sharp enough to shred membranes or peel claws to the bone. The nearest safe route was half a league west.

"We go straight down," Srezzig declared. "If you can't keep up, you'll feed the next clutch."

Drozkax snapped at his tail, but Srezzig had already committed. His descent was controlled chaos—half skid, half fall, all instinct—yet every movement drove him toward the next handhold or outcropping.

Ukshagg waited just long enough to calculate the wind's shift—three heartbeats—then followed, careful and angled, hugging the slope to reduce drag.

Hashaezkend froze at the edge, breath thin, then leapt with a choked sound. Her wings snapped open at the last possible moment, jarring her but slowing her enough to land in one trembling piece.

Shrarzeth tried to mimic Srezzig's reckless dive, but a crosswind caught her midair and spun her sideways. She bounced once, twice—sharp impacts cracking the frost under her body—then flapped hard, forcing her limbs to cooperate. At the bottom she rolled, stood, and shook ice from her bronze scales. Fresh scrapes along her belly oozed for only a moment, then the skin knitted itself shut, the raw pink turning to new bronze before the ice could even melt.

Drozkax went last—not from fear, but from strategy. He watched the others blunder, gauging the timing, then launched himself with the confidence of someone who believed the mountain owed him its respect. He glided the first third, let gravity devour the rest, and slammed into the landing with a victorious snarl.

Below, the five wyrmlings regrouped on a ledge barely wide enough for three. The valley split the earth beneath them, a long fault pressed open and left to weather. Far below, faint white shapes moved in clustered formations—blink rams, scraping lichen from the snow with hooves hard as obsidian and eyes that shimmered with magic.

Ukshagg spoke first, her voice low but decisive. "There's a pack near the icefall. Twenty, maybe more. If we split their flank, we can drive the slowest to the edge."

"Or we hit the strongest head-on," Srezzig countered. "No point culling the weak if we want a real test."

"Easy for you to say," Hashaezkend muttered. "You're not the one who almost fell."

Srezzig ignored her. "Bronze, you're with me. Gold and pearl, circle wide and push them back if they bolt. Drozkax—high side. Cut off their retreat."

Drozkax's eyes narrowed, but even he couldn't deny the logic. He nodded once, a tight jerk, and cracked his knuckles.

Ukshagg and Hashaezkend exchanged a glance, then began moving west, skirting the jagged edge of the icefield. Srezzig and Shrarzeth slipped into the cliff's shadow, navigating old kill sites littered with shattered bone and frozen fur, every sense sharpened for movement, for danger, for the first sign of prey—or rivals.

They made it halfway across the slope before the wind shifted—sharp and traitorous—carrying their scent straight into the rams' nostrils. The prey froze, ears rigid, eyes widening. Then the herd exploded into motion.

Srezzig hissed, "Now," and the clutch sprang.

Hashaezkend faltered on takeoff, her wings catching the wrong angle and buckling under a crosscurrent. Ukshagg saw it a heartbeat before disaster, banked hard, and shoved the pearl forward with a slam of her shoulder that cost her own momentum.

Drozkax, already at full speed, barreled straight into the center of the fleeing pack. Two rams flew sideways, spinning across the snow like kicked stones.

Srezzig didn't spare them a glance. His focus had narrowed, sharpened to a single target—the biggest ram on the ridge. It blinked out of existence, vanishing in a crackle of ozone, then reappeared five yards ahead. But Srezzig saw the air thin and shimmer five yards ahead—a momentary ghost. He adjusted mid-stride, launched for that spot, and caught one horn in his jaws as the ram materialized.

It was like clamping his teeth around a frozen thunderbolt. The horn tasted of ice and ozone; the ram vibrated with every frantic heartbeat. Srezzig wrestled it sideways, dodging its bone-hard hooves, and twisted until something in the neck gave with a dense, wet snap.

Shrarzeth, meanwhile, had taken down a smaller ram with feral enthusiasm, tearing at its throat in wild, joyful bursts. She didn't kill clean, but she killed quick—and with no hesitation at all.

Drozkax landed atop a third, using sheer weight, rage, and momentum to crush it into the snow. When the ram kicked, he erupted into a triumphant scream, tightening his grip until its struggles stilled.

Ukshagg and Hashaezkend worked like a machine with mismatched parts but startling efficiency: Ukshagg forced a panicked ram toward a narrowing ledge, cutting off every escape route. Hashaezkend slipped around its flank and delivered the killing bite with trembling precision. For one breathless instant, the pearl forgot to be afraid.

The fight was over before the echoes of the first snarls faded from the ravine.

When the last ram collapsed, Srezzig scanned the incline, chest heaving. All siblings stood—some bloodied, some shaking, but alive. Steam rose from the fresh kills, turning the snow pink and hot against the bitter air. The wind howled through the ravine, carrying the scent of blood and the echo of violence.

Ukshagg spoke first, voice cool and clinical. "We took five. Two of them are the largest."

Hashaezkend slumped atop her kill, panting but uninjured. "We did it," she whispered, then softer still, "I did it."

Drozkax had already torn into his ram, gore coating his snout. He looked up, spat bone fragments, and growled, "Told you I'd be the best."

Srezzig ignored the posturing. He hooked his claws into his ram's horn and dragged it toward the others. "We bring them back," he said. "No one returns empty."

Shrarzeth bounced forward, muzzle dripping red. "I got the heart!" she crowed, holding the steaming organ high like a trophy.

High above, Shyvnir circled once—silent, immense. She didn't land. Didn't praise. But as her shadow swept across the clutch, dark and vast as a stormcloud, every wyrmling stood a little taller.

They'd earned the next day.

Srezzig watched the sky long after Shyvnir vanished, his chest rising and falling with something heavier than pride. A new understanding settled in him—not pride, but something colder. His siblings had hesitated. They always hesitated. "Next time," he murmured, "I won't wait for them."

But not today.

For now, the five of them huddled close, bodies pressed together against the slicing wind, guarding their hard-won kill from the world and anything bold enough to steal from them. Blood steamed in the cold. Frost gathered on their claws. And none of them pulled away.

Srezzig tore into the ram's flank, and the taste of hot blood and wild herbs flooded his senses.

Nothing had ever tasted so alive.

The climb back up the scree was a silent, brutal affair. They hauled the carcasses onto the ledge and let them drop in a heavy heap, the scent of blood sharp in the cold. Srezzig's ram was the heaviest, a fact that earned him a venomous glare from Drozkax.

"You only got that one because we drove it to you," the black wyrmling snarled.

"And you got yours because you stumbled on it," Srezzig retorted, not looking up from the kill.

Drozkax lunged, not at Srezzig, but at Hashaezkend, slamming her aside. "Try not to trip over your own feet next time."

Before Hashaezkend could scramble back up, Srezzig was between them, wings flared. "Enough. Save it." His voice was low and even, but the spines on his neck were rigid.

Drozkax bared his teeth, but the exhaustion in his own limbs won the argument. He stalked to the far side of the ledge to tear into his kill alone. The clutch ate with brutal efficiency, ripping meat into steaming strips. For the first time, they tasted something other than what their mother provided. They tasted survival. As the heat spread from his belly to his wingtips, Srezzig felt the day's true lesson settle in his bones: they had not only survived the hunt, but each other. For now.

Chapter 4: The Storm's Fury

The wind went from bad to worse in seconds—vicious gusts slicing through scales and wings like blades, each one driving freezing rain into the gaps between their scales like splinters of ice forced under a fingernail. They were flung across the sky like pebbles skimming the surface of water, bodies twisting and spinning against a backdrop of black, roiling clouds. Direction no longer existed—only the frantic burn of muscles, the ragged flutter of wings, and the desperate fight not to be torn apart.

They'd begun in a V-formation: Srezzig at the front, Ukshagg three lengths off his right, Hashaezkend to the left, Shrarzeth tucked behind her with bronze scales catching what little light broke through, and Drozkax brooding at the far edge. Below them, the Fallen Scale Peaks dropped away into churning valleys of mist and the brutal plunge of the Windscour Cliffs. Ahead, storm clouds stacked higher and higher, darker and closer, and something deep in their bones started to hum.

Srezzig felt it first. Not fear—electricity. It crawled up his spine, crackling between the plates of his scales. He felt like a spark about to ignite. His heart struck his ribs in uneven bursts, wings beating harder than the wind demanded. The air itself seemed to shimmer around him. Every breath filled his chest too full, and his mouth tasted like cold metal.

Ukshagg banked closer, wings snapping sharply with each adjustment. For a split heartbeat, Srezzig caught her expression—pure, unbroken focus, eyes reading the storm like a map. She was already planning her exit if the formation failed. And it would. Soon.

Hashaezkend struggled behind her, pale wings straining for any lift they could steal. The updrafts here were weak and choppy, and she looked like a single bad gust might tear her straight off the line. Her jaw trembled, the ridges along her neck quivering with exhaustion.

Shrarzeth, bronze scales barely hardened, fought to stay aloft. Her wings were smaller than the others', every flap scraping at her reserves. She kept glancing toward Hashaezkend's shaking silhouette, teeth gritted, refusing to fall back even as the storm battered her sideways.

Drozkax flew in their shadow, the black membranes of his wings already showing small rips from his usual recklessness. He tested each beat with impatience, skimming the edge of control; twice he shot past Srezzig, a blur of contempt straining against the formation.

Lightning split the horizon. Srezzig's scales crackled in response.

The storm hit them like a wall. Their V-formation shattered instantly. Ukshagg and Drozkax spun off in opposite directions, wings flailing against the violent currents. Srezzig buried his head into the wind and pushed through every brutal twist, his half-healed shoulder screaming with each beat. The membrane there was still raw, and every stroke felt like being torn open again.

Sideways rain slammed into them, freezing where the wind stripped away their warmth. Hashaezkend's voice tore through the chaos: "I'm losing lift!"

Srezzig glanced back. She was below them, wings fluttering uselessly against the downdraft. He banked hard, dropped toward her, and roared, "Bank left! Stay on my tail!"

Ukshagg shot into his slipstream. "We need altitude!"

"Not yet!" Srezzig snapped. "Hold the line!"

Shrarzeth's small body shuddered in the slipstream, frost bristling across her scales. She angled in beside Hashaezkend, matching her desperate wingbeats, eyes wide with terror—and with stubborn, unyielding determination.

Drozkax ignored them all. He folded his wings and dropped like a stone, then shot back up on a razor-thin vertical current. "Cowards!" he screamed, lightning flickering across his tattered membranes like fractured veins of fire.

Srezzig moved on instinct. "Pearl, stick with me! Bronze, follow!" He opened his jaws and released a thin arc of electricity, a bright line carving through the storm. It hummed along the edge of an updraft, glowing like a beacon. For one brief moment, the storm lit up from within.

Ukshagg caught the trail immediately. Shrarzeth and Hashaezkend dove in behind her, clawing for every scrap of lift. Srezzig's shoulder burned like something trying to tear free, but he barely felt it—every beat was agony, but stopping wasn't an option.

The wind howled. The howl of the wind became a physical blow, erasing all sight and thought.

Ahead, Drozkax rode a rolling wave of cloud, letting the storm surge beneath him. Another flash revealed a fresh rip in his wing, dark fluid trailing behind like ink in water. He moved through the storm like something possessed, half feral, half fearless.

Ukshagg's voice cut through the gale: "Trajectory shift! Drozkax is losing lift!"

Too late. Drozkax spun straight into Ukshagg's path, missing her by inches. A vicious gust caught him and sent him spiraling—once, twice, three times—before he snapped himself upright with a violent jerk.

"Idiots!" Srezzig roared. "You'll kill us all before we even reach the cliffs!"

"No," Ukshagg replied, calm as bedrock, "but the probability of casualties is high. Statistically, Drozkax falls first. Then you."

Srezzig answered by firing another arc from his jaws—wider, brighter— cutting a blazing path through the chaos. Ukshagg latched onto it like a lifeline, pulling Shrarzeth and Hashaezkend with her. The bronze wyrmling's wing shook like a leaf, but fear kept her moving.

"I've got you!" Srezzig shouted to Hashaezkend. He dropped lower, pressing his side beneath her failing wings, breaking the wind for her. It cost him altitude and two broken claws, but she stayed airborne.

The storm closed around them. No way around it—only straight through. Thought deserted him—there was only the next wingbeat, and the next, and the lightning he could feel in his teeth before it struck. But behind him, five bodies held formation.

"Hold the line!" he roared. "Brace—"

Lightning slammed into Ukshagg's wing, a blinding blast that lit her bones through her scales. The shockwave struck them a heartbeat later.

Ukshagg tumbled into Srezzig's slipstream; he caught her, shoved her back into place with a grunt.

Shrarzeth screamed, her small bronze body trembling but intact. Drozkax clawed his way back to the line, laughing wildly through the storm. "Still alive, blue?"

Srezzig spat one final arc, blazing a last thread of light through the dark. Five shapes locked in—Srezzig at the front, Ukshagg tight on his right, Hashaezkend and Shrarzeth holding left and rear, Drozkax clinging to the outer edge. For one perfect second, there was no wind, no sound—just five hearts defying the storm.

Then the backwash hit, and they tumbled out of the clouds, battered but breathing.

No one spoke for a long time. Then Srezzig gasped, "Formation. Now. Before the wind eats us."

No one argued. Not even Drozkax.

They locked back into formation and tore across the sky. And for the first time, Srezzig understood what it meant to lead.

The storm hit them with everything it had. Hailstones hammered against their scales and punched straight through the thin skin of their wings. Their V-formation wobbled, trembling on the edge of collapse. All Srezzig could feel was the burning pain in his shoulder and the frantic beat of his wings as he fought to keep everyone together.

Ukshagg's eyes went wide as she read the wind. "It's shifting! We need to climb now or we're done!"

"Hold steady!" Srezzig shouted back. "There's an updraft coming—I can feel it—"

But Hashaezkend was faltering. Every hailstone tore new holes in her wings, tiny at first but widening with each desperate flap. When Srezzig looked back, he saw her eyes—huge, dark, terrified. Her mouth opened in a scream with no sound at all as the air simply... vanished beneath her. And she dropped.

Srezzig didn't think. He banked hard and dove after her, the wind nearly ripping his wings clean off. He tucked, rolled, and shot up beneath her tumbling body. His jaws clamped onto her foreleg. "Lock talons!" he barked.

She couldn't. She froze, paralyzed with fear.

Shrarzeth—bronze scales gleaming even in the storm's chaos, wild eyes blazing—dived from the opposite side and grabbed Hashaezkend's other leg. Srezzig twisted his body until their talons locked together. Between the two of them, they forced Hashaezkend's wings open against the tearing wind.

For one endless moment, they were just three bodies tangled together, falling through nothing.

Drozkax tried to mimic Srezzig's rescue dive, a clumsy, arrogant imitation that sent him plowing straight into Ukshagg's slipstream instead. The impact tore across her gold wing membrane with a sound that made Srezzig's teeth ache. Ukshagg twisted away in time, but fresh cuts raked across her wing.

Srezzig snapped his jaws open with a crack like breaking wood. "GET IN FORMATION!" A jagged bolt of electricity burned from his mouth with the words, singeing the scales near Drozkax's nose. The black wyrmling's wings folded for a heartbeat before he slipped grudgingly back into place, snorting his disdain.

Ukshagg beat her wings hard to regain altitude. Shrarzeth, pressed tight against Hashaezkend's back, flew with raw desperation.

Srezzig locked eyes with Hashaezkend. Her terror was dragging them all down, but he refused to let go. He set a rhythm—one, two, three, four—each beat fighting the spin, hauling them slowly upward.

Lightning turned the night into a white, blinding world. The air tasted like metal and burnt feathers. Srezzig's shoulder was bleeding again, warm against the freezing rain, but he shoved the pain aside.

"Ukshagg, get above us!" he shouted. "We need your slipstream!"

Ukshagg angled down to intercept. Drozkax followed with that twisted grin still carved across his muzzle.

The wind tore through them from a new angle. The formation came apart again.

Srezzig felt Hashaezkend tear free again, caught her with his back leg, and twisted with the current instead of against it. Behind them, Shrarzeth—half their size but stubborn as stone—dug her claws into the ridges along Srezzig's tail and held on, anchoring them, keeping them from spinning into oblivion.

They reformed around Ukshagg, missing a jagged rock spire by mere inches. Below, the cliff faces spun close enough to scrape with a claw.

Srezzig's throat felt raw as he roared, "UP!" His wings hammered the air, lifting not just himself but dragging the entire formation upward with him. Shrarzeth's small body trembled with effort, but her wingbeats matched his perfectly, stubborn and precise.

The hail grew larger—fist-sized stones that tore clean through the membrane under Srezzig's shoulder. Drozkax's flank streaked red. Hashaezkend's right wing barely held shape. But still, somehow, they climbed.

"If you hadn't slowed—" Drozkax snarled.

"If you'd kept formation—" Srezzig snapped back.

Ukshagg—thinking even now—cut clean through their shouting. "The storm's a spiral. It's pulling us toward the center. If we dive through it, we can break out faster—"

Electricity shivered between Srezzig's teeth. "You want us to dive into the heart of it? Where the lightning hits hardest?"

"It's that or die here," Ukshagg said, calm as stone.

Drozkax's grin split wide and savage. "I'm in."

Shrarzeth looked at Srezzig. She was shaking, scales rimed in frost, but she nodded. Without a word, she tucked herself beside him—bronze pressed against blue.

He banked, dropped, and they dove.

Air pressure crushed them instantly. Rain turned to needles of ice. Thunder cracked through the world like a mountain splitting in half.

Halfway down, a lightning strike flashed too close—Srezzig went blind for a heartbeat. He flew by instinct alone. A brutal downdraft slammed into him and Hashaezkend, tearing their grip apart and flinging them sideways.

Shrarzeth dove after them, claws reaching through the blur. Srezzig fought the drag of the wind, forced his wings open despite the agony screaming through his shoulder, and lunged. He caught Shrarzeth's tail, the impact yanking them together. He spun toward Hashaezkend, talons outstretched—

A hailstone the size of his head smashed into his ribs. Pain exploded. He spun helplessly through the storm.

Hashaezkend tumbled away, wings flapping uselessly in the downdraft. Srezzig roared, dove again, and caught the very tip of her tail, hauling her close with a desperate jerk. Shrarzeth dropped from above, slamming into them both—her tiny claws locking onto their scales, anchoring the three of them into one tangled mass of wings and limbs.

Lightning opened around them—an entire corridor of crackling blue-white, a horizontal tunnel of raw fire cutting through the storm. The world went incandescent. At the far edge, Drozkax and Ukshagg flickered in and out of sight, silhouettes against the blaze.

"Don't let go!" Srezzig screamed.

"I... can't..." Hashaezkend whimpered, her wings collapsing.

"Hold on!" he roared back, voice breaking under the storm's fury.

Ahead, a wall of raw, blinding energy blocked their path. Ukshagg—wings spread impossibly wide—braced against it, her entire body arcing with current. The barrier warped under her weight, bending, splitting, and finally forcing open a narrow tunnel just wide enough for the clutch to slip through.

"Now!" Ukshagg's voice crackled like live wire.

Srezzig shoved Hashaezkend forward, using his own body as a shield as he plunged after her. The barrier slapped against their scales, burning nerves numb and sparking along their wings. Behind them, Drozkax hurtled through with a triumphant shriek, sounding disturbingly like he was enjoying himself. Shrarzeth clung to Ukshagg's draft—tiny, fierce, refusing to be shaken loose.

They burst into calm air. Five wyrmlings tumbled free of the storm's jaws, scattered, then caught their individual wind lines to level out.

For ten long heartbeats, no one spoke.

Then Srezzig rasped, "Status?" His shoulder burned like molten stone, but there was a dangerous gleam in his eyes.

Ukshagg flexed her torn wing, testing the membrane. "Functional," she said, steady as ever. "But we fly now, or we die here."

Not a single claw rose in protest.

The sky betrayed them without warning.

One moment—pure chaos: ice daggers, screaming winds, the storm trying to tear their wings from their bodies. The next—nothing. A dead and eerie silence, like the storm had been swallowed whole by something older and hungrier. The hail that had been hammering their scales simply stopped. The sideways sheets of rain dissolved into lingering vapor, misting their wings before vanishing into a stillness that felt deeply wrong.

Srezzig pushed the clutch forward. Everything hurt—wings, throat, bones—but he couldn't let them unravel now. His chest burned with every breath as he fixed his eyes on a narrow strip of horizon ahead.

Ukshagg slid behind him, matching his pace, every wingbeat deliberate and precise. She catalogued the damage—Drozkax's shredded membrane, Hashaezkend's frayed wing edges, Shrarzeth's trembling feathers—and adjusted her rhythm to keep them in one cohesive pattern.

Hashaezkend held position beside Srezzig, her whole body shaking but refusing to drop. She'd lost her voice; only a ragged, hollow breath escaped her throat.

Shrarzeth, bronze scales crusted with ice, tucked herself close behind Hashaezkend. She was the smallest, battered to nearly breaking, but a fierce, stubborn fire still burned in her. When Drozkax drifted back, his usual swagger dimmed by pain, she caught his hungry grin and flashed him one of her own—sharp, defiant.

Five wyrmlings resolved into a single living arrow, wings overlapping and currents shared, cutting cleanly through the thinning air.

They burst through the storm's final breath at full speed. Darkness gave way to a blinding stretch of blue. In an instant, the world fell quiet again.

For a moment, no one dared move.

Srezzig banked slowly, letting the wind carry them. His heart still hammered, but the immediate danger had passed. He kept his voice steady—for Hashaezkend's sake as much as his own.

Hashaezkend let out a broken breath, half-sob, half-laugh. "We... did it?"

Srezzig didn't answer right away. He just flew, giving her time to breathe, to feel the air under her wings again. Shrarzeth gasped beside her, her small chest heaving with effort.

Ukshagg's voice finally cut through their panting. "We're all still airborne, but barely. These wings won't last another hour. We need to land soon—or we're going down."

Drozkax flexed a scarred wing and snorted. "You said I'd drop first."

Ukshagg shrugged, expression unreadable. "Probability. Not destiny. Srezzig changed the math."

They all turned toward him.

He let a tired, proud grin pull at the edge of his jaw. "We're still breathing. Hold formation. We finish this."

Hashaezkend drifted closer. Shrarzeth pressed her chin gently against Srezzig's shoulder—bronze meeting blue, battered but unbroken.

Their wings beat on.

Ukshagg locked into position on Srezzig's right, Drozkax settling on the outer wing with a rough snap of torn membrane. Five wyrmlings carved through the open sky—battered, bleeding, half-frozen, but still flying. The storm behind them shrank into a distant bruise on the horizon, fading from terror into memory. Ahead stretched nothing but empty air, bright and unforgiving, and the barest chance to make it.

Srezzig felt it then—subtle at first, then undeniable. The clutch wasn't just flying in the same direction; they were moving as one. Wings beat in unintentional rhythm, breaths syncing, instincts weaving together into something sharper than fear and stronger than blood. They'd survived something no hatchling should've lived through. They weren't just a clutch anymore. They were becoming something else. Something real. Something fierce.

Whatever came next, Srezzig already knew the shape of it: seven sets of wings cutting the same wind, seven minds reaching the same conclusion a half-breath before it needed to be spoken.

Chapter 5: The Crossroads of Fate

Srezzig slammed down onto the high plateau, spitting grit as the impact rattled his bones. Before the dust even settled, Ukshagg was already perched on a boulder, wings folded with maddening precision, her eyes scanning the horizon. Her perfect landing was a stark contrast to Hashaezkend, who tumbled through frost-burnt grass and flailed upright, mortified. Drozkax made his entrance with pure violence, letting the wind hurl him against the plateau's edge. He bounced, grinning as he flaunted a split wing membrane seeping thin blue lines of blood. Last came Shrarzeth, circling them all with her head low and nostrils flaring before touching down silently at Srezzig's side, her gold eyes sharp and matronly.

Shrarzeth moved between them with practiced ease, her bronze scales catching the harsh light like hammered metal. She pressed her snout to Srezzig's torn wing and breathed out a shimmer that smelled faintly of copper and rain. Tissue knit together beneath her touch, cells pulling tight and weaving closed. She licked along Hashaezkend's scars, her saliva glowing green where it touched damaged flesh. When she reached Drozkax, he growled but didn't move, enduring as her tail coiled around his torn wing, pulsing with amber light that sealed the bleeding. With each wyrmling she healed, her own scales dimmed, as though she were pouring pieces of herself into them.

Hashaezkend leaned against her, a soft trill humming warm between them. Even Drozkax—pretending disinterest—tested his once-ruined wing and muttered, "Not bad," which, coming from him, might as well have been a serenade. Srezzig only bowed his head to her.

It was enough.

Everything went still.

Three paths stretched away from the broken ledge where they'd crash-landed.

The mountain pass carved a narrow wound between two massive granite walls streaked with rust-red minerals. Steep, treacherous, always shifting—loose rocks tumbled like broken teeth with every gust. Wind screamed through the gap, carrying something that sounded disturbingly like warnings.

The forest was a wall of shadow. Gnarled trunks twisted together so tightly that even the bravest light couldn't slip through. Sharp-edged leaves rustled overhead—soft, steady, unnatural—even though no wind touched the ground below. Darkness pooled beneath the branches like a living thing.

The desert stretched bone-white and endless, the horizon shimmering in heat that made the land look fluid. Rocks looked half-melted, their edges warped by centuries of sun that had long stopped showing mercy. Salt crystals glittered like crushed glass beneath the glare.

Srezzig pressed a claw to his bleeding shoulder, watching the wind steal the red droplets before they hit the ground. "Choose." His gaze stayed locked on the mountain pass.

Ukshagg was already pacing, tail twitching as she kicked up dust. "Mountain's the shortest—updrafts at the saddle could lift us two body-lengths a second. But the other side is a vortex of crosswinds." She dragged a claw through the sand, sketching a rough curve. "Winds get chaotic. Forest gives cover, less exposure, but we'd move slow. Desert's the fastest for flying—except dehydration will kill you before anything else does. And the Undragons? They hunt low. I've never seen one in the forest."

Drozkax snorted, wings flaring just for show. "Mountain, then. Only cowards hide in trees." He shot Srezzig a look sharp enough to cut stone.

Srezzig shrugged, unamused. "Fine. You can test those updrafts first—see how you taste to an Undragon."

Drozkax's grin widened, all teeth and arrogant delight. "Try me."

Hashaezkend edged forward, claws trembling. Something beneath the dust caught her talon. She crouched, unearthed it, and lifted it carefully—both claws shaking. A scale. Blackened, twisted like it had burned from the inside out. The edges curled and warped. The stench rising from it was ozone and rot.

Ukshagg took it, turning it over with clinical precision. "This isn't normal decay. Maybe a defect in the clutch?" She sniffed again, visibly unsettled.

Hashaezkend shook her head, voice tight as a pulled tendon. "No. It's… wrong. It feels like it's watching us."

Shrarzeth stepped closer, nostrils flaring. "Wrong doesn't begin to cover it. Desert heat should burn scales to nothing. This is fresh." Her gaze slid to the horizon. "And the last clutch vanished out there."

Drozkax rolled his eyes hard enough to make his spines rattle. "The last clutch was weak. We're not."

Ukshagg set the fragment down, pulling her claws back from its lingering heat. "It's still warm—and the sun isn't even up. Whoever dropped this was here recently."

Srezzig paced in a slow circle around them, eyes on the shimmering horizon. "We stay together. We pick the safest route. Split up and you die for nothing."

Drozkax sneered. "Safety's for prey."

Hashaezkend's tail twitched. "Stupidity's for an Undragon's dinner."

A new smell rolled in with the next gust—sickly sweet rot, like flowers left to decay in the sun.

Ukshagg breathed it in, frowning. "Forest should smell like pine. Not this."

Hashaezkend shuddered. "Smells like clutch rot. Or spoiled milk."

Drozkax snapped his jaws, the crack echoing off stone. "I'll clear the pass myself."

Before he could charge, Srezzig stepped in and dragged his tail through the dust, carving a line between them. "Group decision."

He studied each route: the jagged mountain pass, the suffocating forest, the glittering white desert. His injured wing throbbed behind him. "Mountain risks storms. Desert is slow torture and probably death. The forest..." He hesitated. "Something's wrong with the forest."

Shrarzeth slammed a claw into the ground. "Wrong how? It's silent—no birds, no prey, no creaking branches. Nothing. Dead silence. And that smell?" She glared at Drozkax. "Charging into the pass because you're too proud to think—*that's* the cowardice."

Ukshagg tapped her claws together, mind racing. "Forest is seventy-eight percent safer statistically. Even with the smell. And Undragon sightings drop to almost nothing under thick canopy."

Drozkax spat dust but didn't argue. He stared at the mountain like it had personally offended him.

Hashaezkend quickly buried the scale fragment again, sweeping sand over it until it vanished.

Shrarzeth stared at the forest edge with narrowed eyes. "I don't trust that silence. Something's in those shadows. If we go in there, we're walking straight into its mouth."

They all went quiet, listening. No rustling leaves. No chittering insects. No breath of movement. Only the distant hiss of blowing sand.

Ukshagg summed it up plainly: "Forest gives us the best chance. Pass is fastest. Desert is death."

Drozkax stepped closer to Srezzig, claws flexing. "Cowards."

Srezzig showed every tooth. "Brave enough to survive."

Hashaezkend's ears flattened tight against her head. She looked between the mountain, the desert, and the forest—then back at the forest. "I don't know what's wrong. But it's more than the smell or that scale. It feels like something's watching from the dark."

Ukshagg nodded once. Drozkax turned away, scowling at the granite ridges as if he could intimidate them into submission.

Srezzig let out a long breath and faced the forest's shadowed maw. "We choose together. We fly together. Today, nobody dies alone."

But the crushing silence—and the prickling certainty that something in the trees was already aware of them—followed them as they prepared to enter.

As Ukshagg laid out the grim probabilities, Srezzig found his attention snagged by the rock face. The granite was carved with wild, vicious gashes—too massive, some dug so deep the stone looked melted at the edges. "Not natural," he muttered.

"There's more," Hashaezkend whispered, her voice tight. She led them to a cluster of stones near the desert's edge, half-fused together as if by blistering heat. But it was what she unearthed from the dust that silenced them all: a blackened, twisted scale that radiated a faint warmth and the stench of ozone and rot.

"It feels like it's watching us," she said, claws trembling.

Shrarzeth's nostrils flared. "It hunts because it hates. It will drive us toward death in the pass or trap us in the trees. Pick your poison."

Drozkax scraped a claw across the melted rock. "We fight it. We're stronger."

"The last clutch was strong, too," Ukshagg said, her voice flat. "This thing is tracking us. The forest will mask our scent and muffle our sound."

Srezzig looked from the treacherous pass to the shadowed maw of the forest. He picked up a fragment Drozkax had kicked loose—not a scale, but a glossy, hollow fang, still faintly warm. Dread coiled in his stomach. "Forest," he said, his voice final. "We stay together. No one falls behind."

Drozkax stomped the ground. "So we hide?" he barked, unleashing a stream of hissing acid that burned clean through a nearby boulder. "We should be fighting whatever's out there."

Ukshagg rolled her eyes. "That's what the last clutch tried. You remember how many wings they came back with? None."

Hashaezkend sat hunched at the far edge of the plateau, wings wrapped tight around herself, eyes darting between the group and the forest below. Every so often she flinched, like something unseen kept brushing past her.

A sudden gust slammed into them, hard enough to stagger Drozkax. It carried a sound with it—not quite a roar, not quite a scream. More like metal scraping metal, twisted and furious. It came from the mountain pass and echoed far longer than it should have, rattling every rock face.

Hashaezkend went rigid. "That's not wind."

Ukshagg's voice dropped flat. "Seismic resonance. Something big. Moving fast."

Cold dread washed over Srezzig. He scanned the pass, then the desert, then the forest—feeling every option sharpen into a blade. Pride told him to take the pass: get it done fast, prove they could handle whatever came. But that shriek, those burn marks, the molten scars in the stone, the way every scale on his spine stood on end—all of it pointed to the forest. The smarter choice. The alive choice.

He set his jaw and faced them. "We're taking the forest. No arguments."

Drozkax inhaled like he was ready to spit fire, but another shriek—closer now, angrier—split the air, and his mouth snapped shut.

Ukshagg was already moving. "Seventy-nine percent now. The delay bought us an extra point."

Srezzig exhaled slowly, grounding himself. "Hashaezkend, you're up front. Slowest sets the pace."

She blinked at him. "Why me?"

His answer was simple and merciless. "Because if you fall behind, we all die."

The pearl wyrmling nodded, looking smaller for a moment—but sharper, too. Focused.

Ukshagg took the rear, eyes locked on the pass. Drozkax went second, shoulders hunched, radiating frustration with every step. Shrarzeth drifted close to Srezzig—closer than usual—so close their wings nearly brushed. Her bronze scales shimmered faintly, catching the dying light, as if refusing to show fear even when her heartbeat stuttered against her ribs.

Everything felt too quiet. Every sound was amplified—claws scraping stone, wings rustling, the faint hiss of Drozkax's acid still eating through rock.

They reached the forest edge just before the next shriek. This one rose from behind them, sharper, layered—*more than one.* Something—no, *multiple somethings*—were moving across the stone at a speed that made Srezzig's scales tighten.

He didn't hesitate. "Go!"

The clutch plunged into the trees, weaving between trunks, keeping low to the ground.

The darkness swallowed them whole. Every few steps, Srezzig caught flickers at the edge of his vision—shapes that vanished when he looked directly at them. Maybe shadows. Maybe not. He forced himself forward, lungs burning, one eye fixed on the rear, counting heartbeats between each distant shriek.

Hashaezkend found her pace quickly, surprisingly smooth, setting a rhythm that was fast but manageable. Drozkax kept glancing over his shoulder, muttering curses under his breath.

From the rear, Ukshagg's voice threaded through the dark—low, steady, precise. "Sharp left in ten. Hit the ground when we reach the clearing. Don't look up."

Srezzig didn't question her. He followed each command the moment she gave it.

The first clearing was wrong.

As they broke through the treeline, a stench hit them—burnt meat, crackling ozone, and something sickly sweet underneath, like rotting honey. The ground was littered with scale fragments. Some were old enough to have fused into the dirt; others looked freshly shed, still glossy around the edges.

At the clearing's center yawned a pit, four body-lengths across, ringed with blackened wood and blistered stone.

Hashaezkend stopped at the edge, looking back at Srezzig with wide, uncertain eyes.

He studied the pit. He couldn't see the bottom—just heat rising in shimmering waves, warping the air above it.

Ukshagg skidded to his side, breath sharp. "Don't stop. That's not just a pit—it's a vent."

Srezzig nodded and motioned Hashaezkend left. The clutch skirted the edge, claws sinking into soft, scorched soil that smelled like lightning and ash. Drozkax lingered, peering into the darkness like he expected something to leap out.

"Move," Srezzig ordered, sharper this time.

Drozkax obeyed—but not before spitting a sizzling glob of acid into the vent, listening for the hiss as it vanished into the depths.

They pushed deeper into the forest. The shrieks from the plateau faded, replaced by a low, unnerving hum that vibrated through the ground, through the roots, through their bones.

"They're following," Ukshagg murmured. "I can feel the shifts in the soil when they move."

Srezzig grunted. "How many?"

She hesitated—a rare thing. "At least two. Maybe more."

Drozkax spat at the ground. "Let them try."

Hashaezkend said nothing, but her whole body trembled, her wings pressed tight against her sides.

Shrarzeth, usually quick with some reckless grin, kept her head down now, tail dragging, scales dulled by fear and exhaustion.

Eventually the hum faded. The air cooled. The trees grew farther apart, and Srezzig allowed them to slow. They were still alive. Still together.

They found shelter—if it could be called that—beneath a tangle of massive roots. Hidden from above, protected on three sides, the space felt tight but defensible.

Ukshagg immediately began checking the perimeter, nose low, sniffing every inch like she could read the earth itself.

Hashaezkend curled up tight, tail curled over her nose, staring at a single patch of soil as though she expected it to shift.

Drozkax paced in jagged lines, restless energy radiating off him, carving deep grooves into the soft wood with his claws.

Srezzig took watch at the entrance, forcing his breath to stay steady. He scanned the darkness beyond the trees, waiting for the next sound, the next shadow, the next threat that would test them all over again.

Time passed—minutes or hours, impossible to tell in the choking quiet.

Hashaezkend broke the silence first. Her voice was barely a breath. "What if it gets in? What do we do?"

Srezzig didn't turn around. He kept watching the treeline, every muscle wired tight. "We fight," he said. "Or we run. Maybe both."

Ukshagg muttered from the rear, her voice low and clinical. "Probability of survival: fifty-three percent... and dropping."

Shrarzeth, curled small at Srezzig's feet, finally whispered, "It's watching. It's always watching." Her bronze scales shivered with each word, as though something cold had brushed along her spine.

Srezzig stared into the night, feeling the weight of every unseen eye—real or imagined—pressing against them. The shadows felt too thick. The silence, too intentional.

"We wait," he said quietly. "And we get through it. Like we always do."

No one answered. No one had to.

Outside, in the dark, something shifted—slow, deliberate—preparing its next move. The forest held its breath, and the world waited with it.

Chapter 6: Into the Heart of the Forest

The forest watched Srezzig. He felt it in the prickling of his scales, a pressure that had nothing to do with the humid air. This wasn't the wrongness of decay, of spores that clogged the nose or bark crumbling to dust. This was the wrongness of being prey.

Every twisted trunk was swollen with knot-clusters shaped like unblinking eyes, sap leaking between them like amber tears. Above, the canopy bent into unnatural arches, the leaves arranged in patterns that made his mind itch—a chaotic language he almost understood. Shadows pooled where light should have been, and the air tasted of copper and old secrets.

He pushed forward through curtains of fern and bramble. Ukshagg followed close behind, her gold scales catching the stray beams of light. Drozkax shoved a thorny branch aside with a growl, while Hashaezkend flinched at the sound. Behind them all, quiet as a drifting ghost, came Shrarzeth.

The forest swallowed them whole. Branches wove so tightly overhead that daylight barely filtered through—just pale ghosts of gold shimmering now and then. The ground was a nightmare: roots tangled like living traps, moss slick as grease, mud grabbing at their talons with every step.

"We should have taken the pass," Drozkax muttered, each word bitten sharp. "This place reeks of rot."

"Actually, it's full of life," Ukshagg corrected, though her voice trembled. "You're smelling fermentation. Decomposition. Entropy."

Srezzig cut them both off. "Eyes forward. Keep it down."

Hashaezkend coughed once. "I think it's watching us."

Nobody disagreed.

The path tightened until they were nearly brushing shoulders. Movement flickered above and behind them—constant now—shadows swimming through the air without ever taking shape. Srezzig kept them moving, but every instinct in him screamed: *run*.

They passed a tree older than anything Srezzig had ever imagined, its trunk fused with stone and thick lichen. Its roots spread outward into a perfect circle of tiny white mushrooms. Srezzig gave it a wide berth, but Hashaezkend's tail brushed the ring—and the spores burst outward in absolute silence. Dust filled the air, each particle catching the dim sunlight and holding it a second too long.

Ukshagg sneezed, a sound like a miniature explosion, then stumbled into a sapling. "Just spores," she mumbled, blinking rapidly—as if naming them made them harmless.

Then came the first whisper: "Ukshagg."

Barely louder than a leaf brushing across scales, but every one of them heard it. They froze.

"Hashaezkend," the whisper breathed again—softer, stretched thin like pulled sugar.

Drozkax bared his teeth. "What's out there? Show yourself!" Acid glands heated beneath his scales.

Srezzig scanned the shadows. At first, nothing—just the usual tricks of dark and darker. Then he saw it: a flicker of pale blue light, gone before he could blink. Then gold. Then pearl. Then black. Each flash closer than the last, each one a perfect mimic of their scale-colors.

The clutch tried to regroup, but the lights were too fast—darting between trees, weaving circles around them, never lingering long enough for anyone to track.

"They're mimicking us," Ukshagg said, her voice trembling. "Matching colors, frequencies—everything."

"They're not copying anything! Watch this!" Drozkax roared.

He launched himself forward—a black blur of rage—at the nearest flicker of blue. The light dodged. Drozkax crashed into a thicket of brambles, and before Srezzig could even shout a warning, the vines writhed to life. They coiled around Drozkax like living ropes, tightening with every furious howl and gout of acid he sprayed. The stench of burning vegetation filled the air, a sickeningly sweet announcement of his failure.

"Drozkax!" Srezzig barked. "Stop before you—"

But the warning came too late.

The other lights surged in, closing fast. Now they hovered—clear as ghosts, unmistakably alive. Each was about the size of a mountain cat, with gossamer wings and grins full of far too many needle-fine teeth.

Ukshagg yelped as a gold-lit fey darted at her snout, nicking her with its claws before veering away again. Hashaezkend tried to make herself small, but three of the creatures swarmed her head, cooing and hissing in voices that almost—*almost*—sounded like theirs.

"Come play," one giggled, pitch sliding like a cracked flute.

"Stay forever," another moaned, stretching the word into something sticky and wrong.

Drozkax thrashed in the brambles, ripping one limb free. He spat a jet of acid at the nearest fey. The creature shrieked—a sound so sharp every bird for a mile went silent—before its body dissolved into a heap of wet, crystalline shards. Before the pieces even settled, the other fey pounced, devouring the remains with frantic, clicking hunger. One of them looked up, a shard of its kin still caught in its teeth, and grinned at Hashaezkend. She shrank back, a whimper caught in her throat, as Ukshagg stared, muttering, "Efficient..."

But the violence changed the forest.

The air thickened. The trees leaned closer, bark creaking like bones shifting. The ground beneath Srezzig writhed—actually *writhed*—before erupting into a nest of green, slick tendrils, each one tipped with a pulsing mouth lined with tiny, grasping suckers.

The vines rose and lunged for them.

Srezzig tried to leap clear, but a vine snapped around his back foot and yanked him off balance. He hit the ground hard. Mud splashed up his snout as he bit at the tendril, but it tasted like slime and rot—bitter enough to make his tongue go numb. Another vine coiled around his wing, wrenching it sideways. Two more wrapped his forelimbs. Within seconds he was pinned belly-down in the muck, unable to move more than an inch.

Hashaezkend screamed. Vines lifted her clean off the ground, flipped her upside down like she weighed nothing, and slammed her into a tree trunk with a crack that sounded like bones breaking. Ukshagg tried using her claws for leverage, muttering calculations through clenched teeth, but for every limb she freed, two more vines slithered around her and cinched tight.

Drozkax went feral. Acid sprayed everywhere, burning vines and fey. A misdirected gout of it splashed across Srezzig's tail, and searing agony shot up his spine. He roared, the sound a mix of fury and pain, as the acid ate through his scales. But for every vine that shriveled, three more burst from the soil to take its place.

"Drozkax, STOP!" Srezzig rasped, but the black wyrmling either couldn't hear him or had lost control entirely. The fey swarmed him in a frenzy, dozens of them, biting and cackling, tugging at his wings and legs until even his fury vanished beneath a writhing mass of glowing wings and whispering teeth.

The clutch was dragged apart—each trapped in their own pocket of darkness, vines coiled around snouts and legs and tails. Immobilized, helpless. Left with just enough air to breathe...and to watch.

Srezzig strained against the binds, trying to bark an order, any order, but the only thing that moved was the vine around his throat. It tightened slowly, relentlessly. His vision flickered, edges blurring. Above him, the fey hovered in drifting rings, their laughter soft and grating, like glass being ground together.

Then the voices began again—no longer whispers from the canopy but full-throated, echoing all around them.

"Hashaezkend," a fey sang, pitch-perfect and mocking. "We see you. We see you."

"Ukshagg," another giggled, weaving loops above her head. "So clever. Can you count all of us now?"

Srezzig tried to roar back, but the vine squeezed his throat tight enough to choke off the sound.

Across the clearing, Drozkax still thrashed, jaws frozen in a permanent snarl, body convulsing under the swarm. Ukshagg had nearly vanished beneath a net of vines and shimmering wings, but Srezzig caught a single glimpse—one gold eye wide and unblinking between the leaves.

Hashaezkend dangled upside down, tail limp, chest spasming with frantic, shallow breaths.

Shrarzeth was gone.

Not hiding. Not struggling.

Just—*gone.*

The fey circled closer, their wings flickering in and out of the dim light like dying stars. One settled on Srezzig's snout, cold feet pricking his scales. It grinned, revealing a mouth full of jagged, crystal fangs, and whispered:

"Your turn soon, Srezzig. The forest always gets what it wants."

Srezzig snapped instinctively, but the fey only laughed and darted away.

The vines tightened, and the darkness closed in around him, patient and deliberate, the way roots find water.

The vines had teeth. Srezzig felt them—barbed ridges that dug deeper with every struggle. He could see Ukshagg nearby, her jaw clenched. Even trapped, her eyes darted methodically, counting the five wraps on her left forelimb, the three around her tail, the one tight as braided wire at her throat. She was cataloging every detail, as if information alone could save her.

Her vision blurred at the edges, but she forced her mind into clarity. The fey swarmed them, maybe a hundred strong, bodies rippling with shifting light. A few hovered close, baring those impossibly wide, hungry grins. The rest flickered at a distance, their colors pulsing every time Drozkax shrieked or Srezzig thrashed.

"Bioluminescent group response," Ukshagg whispered, barely a breath. "Light synced to movement. High reactivity."

One fey darted in, bared every crystalline tooth, and licked her nose. The touch stung—ozone mixed with something sweet and numbing. Her eyes watered, but she pushed past the sensation and re-centered on the pattern.

The vine tightened with each heartbeat, but there was a rhythm: whenever a fey swooped in close, the grip loosened—briefly, deliberately—making space for the kill. If she timed it just right—

There.

A blue fey dove for her muzzle. The vine around her left claw slackened for an instant, and Ukshagg yanked her limb free. Her claws raked the vine's surface. It didn't tear, but it shifted enough to let a sliver of air into her lungs. She reached for her pouch—the one stuffed with scales from past clutches, old specimens, possible catalysts—but the vines had pinned it tight against her ribs.

Across the clearing, Drozkax howled, his whole body convulsing. Acid dripped from his jaw, sizzling holes through the leaves, but the vines seemed to anticipate each movement. They lashed his mouth shut, wrapped his wings flat to his sides, then hoisted him off the ground and dangled him from a low branch like a snarling lantern. He bucked and thrashed until even the fey circling him looked bored.

Srezzig lay pinned belly-down, completely still now. His eyes burned with unspent fury, but all he could do was open and close his jaws in slow, useless motions—like a predator forced to swallow dirt.

Hashaezkend was different.

The pearl wyrmling stopped fighting the moment the vine cinched around her chest. She went limp, letting herself hang even as blood rushed to her head and set her ears ringing. At first the fey swarmed her—licking, nipping, testing her softness—but then one paused. The largest. Its wings shimmered like moonlight on black water. It cocked its head and stared directly into Hashaezkend's wide eyes.

She inhaled shakily—and began to hum.

Not a song exactly, but a low, resonant tone that vibrated through her throat and chest, seeping into the vine wrapped around her torso. The vine shuddered, then loosened. The fey drifted closer, entranced, drawn to the sound like moths to fire.

Ukshagg watched, analyzing every breath Hashaezkend took. Then she tried her own version. "Initiating acoustic trial," she muttered, forcing a low hiss through her teeth, then a series of sharp clicks against her palate, then a guttural growl scraped from deep in her chest.

The vine reacted instantly. Brutal pressure crushed her chest, squeezing the air from her lungs in a single, agonizing spasm. Black spots exploded in her vision, and the world dissolved into a roaring in her ears. Her analysis had been wrong. Fatally wrong.

Hashaezkend didn't break. She kept humming, steady and deliberate, shifting once to add a deeper, resonant note. The nearest fey echoed it perfectly. Then another joined. Then a dozen more. Soon the entire clearing hummed in eerie, shimmering harmony—dozens of voices layering the melody with uncanny precision.

Hashaezkend spoke without moving her jaw, the words vibrating through the tones she held. "We're not here to hurt you. We just need to pass through. Our clutchmate was scared. That's all."

The leader—if that's what the moon-winged fey truly was—floated closer, her wings glimmering like thin silver flames. Her eyes were huge and reflective, pupils contracting into pinpoints. "You burned our kin," she said, her voice less mimic and more... genuine.

Hashaezkend nodded carefully. "They tried to eat us. We reacted."

The fey queen considered her for a long heartbeat, then drifted up to Hashaezkend's ear and whispered, "If you were like the others, you would be dead now." Her smile widened, unsettling but almost beautiful. "But you sing. Sing more."

Hashaezkend inhaled shakily and pushed the hum into actual words. "We are lost. We need safe passage. We are not your enemies."

The queen hovered there, staring into her eyes. Then she flicked her wings once, a decisive motion. The vines around Hashaezkend loosened— only a quarter turn, but enough to drag in a full breath.

"Hashaezkend! Keep doing that. It's working on them," Ukshagg called, her voice thin but determined.

Hashaezkend kept singing.

Drozkax, meanwhile, hadn't stopped fighting. He twisted and bucked until his muscles seized. He spat acid until his jaw trembled from the strain. Then he simply hung there—limbs shaking, breath ragged—as the fey plucked scales from his tail one by one. Each stolen scale was met with a high, delighted giggle.

Even through the pain, Drozkax found Srezzig's face and held it with his eyes.

Srezzig met the look. He saw the fury, the humiliation, the betrayal in those wild black eyes. And for one burning heartbeat, he wanted to unleash every spark in his body—to rip free, to burn this entire haunted forest to ash, to prove dragons were not prey.

But Hashaezkend's humming anchored him. The slow, patient work of her voice. The vines softening in time with her breath. The fey lowering their guard.

Something clicked.

The prey you let walk away had a way of circling back with teeth of its own.

The hum spread wider. The fey chorus thickened, their voices weaving together until the sound echoed through the trees and folded back on itself in layers of shimmering resonance. The vines responded—they stopped tightening, paused, then began to unwind in slow, deliberate pulses. Always in sync with the music. Always to the same rhythm.

Ukshagg finally wrenched her claws free and snagged her pouch. She pulled out a single old gold scale, angling it to bounce a shard of light into the nearest fey's face. It recoiled, hissing, but then its own wings shifted, catching the light and reflecting it back with perfect, unnerving accuracy. Another fey joined the mimicry, then a dozen, until the air was a dizzying web of reflected light, a silent, synchronized mockery of her desperate signal.

Hashaezkend's song shifted again, softer and more layered. The queen picked up the new melody instantly, weaving her voice through it with uncanny precision. The vines around Hashaezkend unwound completely and dropped her onto the soft moss. She didn't move at first—just kept singing, letting the fey drift closer and closer until they circled her like worshippers at an altar.

Srezzig watched it all unfold—awed, irritated, jealous, relieved. Every emotion churned like a storm in his chest. He tried to mimic the sound, but it came out wrong—too sharp, too charged with instinct. The vines around him clenched, unimpressed.

Ukshagg flashed the gold scale again, precise as a signal flare. Then, instead of fighting the vine's strength, she used one claw to make a single, calculated slice along its length. It wasn't a struggle, but a clinical incision.

The vine spasmed, bleeding thick sap, and its grip faltered just enough for her to breathe.

"Srezzig," she called, breath tight. "Try humming—softer. Less threat."

He tried. His first attempt was practically a growl, but the second was closer—a breathy, almost melodic rumble. The vines around him eased a fraction. Enough to matter.

Drozkax remained stubborn, refusing to adjust anything. His vines were the last to respond, constricting until his scales creaked. But even he couldn't resist the tidal pull of the swelling fey chorus; eventually the vines slackened around him as well.

Hashaezkend stood tall now in the center of the clearing, surrounded by fey like a living lantern. She glanced at the others and nodded. "It's working. Keep going."

The vines around Srezzig slithered apart and fell to the ground in defeated curls. He pushed himself upright, pain screaming through his shoulder, but he refused to show it. Ukshagg continued flashing signals with the gold scale, each flick earning a mirrored response from the nearest fey.

Drozkax was last to be released. The fey queen floated to him, whispering a single, sibilant word against the torn edge of his wing that sounded like a secret and a curse. Only then did the vines fall away. He hit the ground hard and rolled to his feet, teeth bared, but the fey only laughed, rising to rejoin the chorus above.

The clutch gathered—battered, scraped, shaken, but alive—while the fey whirled overhead in a vortex of wings and shimmering color. The vines hung slack across the clearing now. Even the earth beneath their claws felt less hostile, as if the forest itself had paused to listen.

Hashaezkend's voice, raw but steady, held the clearing in place.

"We are not your enemies," she said. "Let us go."

Three days after the ambush, the Windscour Cliffs rose like a knife edge against the sky. Every ledge looked ready to crumble, every jutting spike a threat. Centuries of wind had carved the limestone into smooth, deceptive curves—beautiful in a cruel sort of way—yet brittle enough to crack beneath a single misplaced talon. Srezzig hated the place instantly, but that was the point. Nothing weak survived here.

They touched down hard on a narrow shelf barely big enough for all five of them. Srezzig's wings flared and kicked up white dust as he landed with a grunt. Drozkax caught a sideways gust and skidded tail-first across the stone, scattering chalky powder everywhere. Ukshagg banked sharply and landed clean, her claws finding perfect purchase. Hashaezkend and Shrarzeth dropped in together, exchanging a quick, relieved look before ducking behind a low outcrop.

The wind clawed at their wings. Far below, the ocean hammered the cliff base in a relentless rhythm. Nothing surrounded them but raw stone and a long, unforgiving drop. Srezzig shook grit from his frill, glanced upward—and froze.

Something was wrong about the ledge above.

He snapped his tail in warning. The others halted instantly. Ukshagg's eyes narrowed to slits. Drozkax spread his wings, bracing. Hashaezkend pulled Shrarzeth tighter behind the rock, both of them going quiet.

Srezzig edged forward and peered up.

A lone figure crouched on the shelf above—almost invisible against the limestone except for the faint shimmer of its wings and the restless twitch of its tail. At first he assumed rival clutch: territorial, looking for a fight. But then he caught the strange sheen of its scales, the odd, meticulous way it worked at something with clawed hands. Not digging. Not eating.

Building.

"Not a rival," Ukshagg murmured. "Alone. Adult-sized... but coloring is off. Scales catch light wrong."

"Or it's bait," Srezzig muttered. He shot a look at the others. "We go up. Quiet."

Beating against the vicious cliff winds, they climbed—Srezzig first, Ukshagg right behind him, Drozkax following with a snarl on his breath. They landed on the wider shelf in formation, claws spread, heads low.

The figure didn't even glance their way. It kept tapping at a dark pile of twisted scales and glass vials, muttering in an archaic dialect Srezzig half-recognized from old lessons he'd barely passed.

Then it spoke without turning. "I had begun to calculate the odds that you weren't coming."

Ukshagg's wings stiffened. "High-variant speech," she whispered. "Formal register."

A dry, rasping laugh. "I haven't spoken this tongue in seasons. Almost forgot the taste of it."

The figure rose slowly, deliberately.

A dragon.

Taller than Srezzig, lean as a blade. Deep sapphire scales threaded with silver veins. Notches along the neck frill—old bite marks, half-healed. Worn leather gloves covered both hands, each fingertip capped with polished bone. Dark goggles hid its eyes, lenses catching the cliff light like twin shards of ice.

It gave a mocking little bow. "Zaekshilen—healer, archivist, last of the Clutch of Drowned Mirrors. Honored by your arrival."

Srezzig's wings tensed. Ukshagg's mind was clearly racing, every calculation clicking behind her eyes. Drozkax spat and raked his claws across the stone.

Zaekshilen smiled—thin, sharp, all teeth. "You've been standing there long enough to have made an attempt. Since you haven't, you're here for something else. What is it?"

"We came for blink rams," Srezzig said. "This territory was supposed to be empty." His gaze drifted over the scattered scales, vials, and tools. "You Undragon?"

Zaekshilen actually laughed. "If I were, you'd already be dead or corrupted. No—I hunt Undragons. Or what remains of them." He flicked a wing toward the shimmering scales. "These are castoffs. Malformed. Warped."

Ukshagg leaned in, pupils narrowing. "You study corruption?"

"Someone has to," Zaekshilen replied. "Everyone else either runs or fights. I record."

From behind the boulder, Hashaezkend whispered, "Why?"

"Because memory's all we've got," Zaekshilen said, voice steady despite the darkness behind his goggles. "If no one remembers, if no one keeps the stories straight, we're all lost."

Drozkax snorted. "Sounds like fey nonsense. Eat or be eaten—then move on."

Zaekshilen didn't rise to it. "I prefer understanding to devouring. But if you'd rather—" He flexed those bone-tipped claws. "—we can trade."

"We don't need lectures," Srezzig snapped. "Just tell us where the rams are."

Zaekshilen ignored him entirely, zeroing in on Drozkax instead. "You've got traces of corruption on you. Let me see."

Drozkax bristled. "Back off."

Srezzig weighed the archivist's strange calm against the creeping rot on his brother's wing. A known poison was better than a hidden one. He nodded. "Let them look. They're a scholar, not a killer."

With a reluctant, grinding hiss, Drozkax lifted a wing. Dark mottling spread across the membrane in strange filigree patterns. Zaekshilen circled him, studying each line like a map.

"It's begun, but not deep yet," the archivist said. "You're lucky."

Ukshagg stepped closer. "What is it?"

Zaekshilen uncorked a vial and held it up. Inside, a drop of thick black liquid writhed. "Corruption's essence. It spreads through breath and touch. It rewrites scale and mind. Most don't survive the change."

Srezzig's tail swept low against the stone. "So? We're still here."

Zaekshilen angled his head toward him. "You're the first clutch I've seen cross the Scour intact, minds still sharp. That makes you... valuable."

Hashaezkend's feathered mane ruffled. "Are we contagious?"

Zaekshilen shrugged, wings rattling softly. "Can't say. But if you help me, we might discover the truth before it's too late."

Drozkax bared his teeth. "Or you could just point us to the damn rams."

Zaekshilen leaned in, the goggles catching the cliff light like twin suns. "The Undragons hunt the blink rams too. If you want to feast, you help me set a trap. Otherwise the Undragons will use them to hunt you."

Srezzig considered the options—few and ugly—then dipped his head. "We help. Then you take us to the herd."

Zaekshilen's smile sharpened. "Deal."

They huddled together, a tense triangle of clutchmates and archivist. Drozkax kept his tail between Zaekshilen and the others. Ukshagg tracked the archivist's every subtle move. The plan took shape between them, a fragile thing held together by shared hunger and mutual distrust.

They worked through the night—darkness gave them cover, and besides, none of them could stand to sit still. Zaekshilen's "plan" wasn't strategy so much as controlled chaos. Every ten minutes brought something new: another variable, another near-disaster, another reason for the clutch to argue.

Ukshagg thrived on it. She tracked every shift, recalculated every risk, until the numbers began to overlay the mess and form a pattern only she could see. Drozkax hated every second. Each update reminded him how thin the line was between predator and prey. Hashaezkend stayed in the shadows, eyes flicking to Srezzig whenever the wind howled too sharply, taking comfort in the blue's sheer refusal to die.

Srezzig put up with all of it for one reason—the alternative was worse.

Just before dawn, Zaekshilen waved them over. The archivist had rigged a makeshift lab between two leaning slabs of rock, lit by a severed dragon eye suspended in fluid that pulsed sickly green. Spread across a stretched canvas were five "devices"—each barely larger than a talon, wrapped in bone spirals and glass shards. Those vials of black liquid from earlier sat in a neat row, bubbling faintly even at rest.

Zaekshilen tapped the first device. "Sonic emitter. Excites the air around the target and disrupts their nerve patterns. Close range works best."

Ukshagg reached for it, but Zaekshilen whipped it out of her claws. "Not for children. You don't understand the harmonics."

Drozkax snorted. "Give it here. I'll test it on the first Undragon that breathes wrong."

Zaekshilen ignored him and moved to the second device. "Dispersal agent. If you get touched"—a pointed glance at Drozkax's leaking wing membrane—"spray this directly on the wound. Slows the corruption for twelve hours. Maybe."

Hashaezkend looked from her own pale scales to Srezzig's injured shoulder. "And after that?"

Zaekshilen shrugged, a gesture too casual for the topic. "After that, we see what's left."

"You promised us the blink rams," Srezzig growled.

Zaekshilen tilted his head, goggles drinking in the faint light. "If the Undragons don't eat them first."

A sound rippled through the air then—subtle, wrong. A shadow swept across the ledge and vanished into the haze. Srezzig stiffened instantly.

"Single flyer," Ukshagg murmured, scanning the wind currents. "Small. Doesn't match a hunter's silhouette."

Zaekshilen nodded. "Scout. They always send one before the pack. We have minutes. Maybe less."

Drozkax bared his teeth. "Let it come. We'll show it the new harmonics."

But Zaekshilen was already adjusting the sonic emitter, claws moving with elegant precision as he tuned tiny crystalline nodes. Even Ukshagg fell silent watching him work. When he finally held it out, he placed it deliberately into Srezzig's claws. The blue felt the weight, the faint inner hum of magic waiting to be shaped.

"Wait until you see their eyes," Zaekshilen said quietly. "That's the part they hate—the being seen. It's the last bit of real dragon still trapped inside them."

The scout came fast, riding the wind with none of the grace of true flight—just raw, brutal momentum. Its scales were wrong: colorless, like scraped bone, threaded through with veins of shifting shadow. Its head was swollen, twice the proper size, jaw stretched into a permanent scream. It slammed onto the ledge hard enough to punch holes in the stone and fixed its gaze straight on Srezzig.

For a moment, neither of them looked away.

Then Srezzig clicked the device on.

The sound wasn't a sound at all—it was a low, subterranean growl that lived in your bones. The Undragon convulsed, wings folding in on themselves, head whipping back and forth like the air was trying to tear it apart. It howled, and the shriek wasn't just animal—it was grief, rage, memory twisted until only hunger remained.

Drozkax stared, stunned. "It's... beautiful."

"It's a nightmare," Ukshagg shot back. "But it works."

The Undragon staggered, lost its footing, and tumbled over the cliff, falling toward the hammering surf below. Srezzig kept the emitter running until Zaekshilen barked, "Enough! You'll call the rest!"

Hashaezkend sagged, trembling—half relief, half horror.

Zaekshilen dimmed the crystal, then swept a wing across the ledge like sealing a ledger. "That's the new world," he said, voice drained of anything but truth. "That's what the blight does. Turns memory into hunger, and hunger into weapon."

"What causes it?" Ukshagg asked, eyes still on the empty cliff edge.

Zaekshilen straightened the vials in a neat row. "Plague, curse—some blame the old queens, others blame invaders from beyond the Scour. I say it doesn't matter. What matters is surviving what's left."

Srezzig's jaw stayed tight. "And the herd?"

Zaekshilen gestured toward the vast drop and the ridge beyond. "Past the next rise there's a hollow. The blink rams feed at dawn. But the Undragons know that. They'll be waiting. They don't eat anymore—they just like the hunt."

Drozkax spat over the ledge. "Then we beat them to it."

Zaekshilen nodded, satisfied. "When you do, bring back a sample. Flesh, blood—anything that bleeds black or moves when it shouldn't."

Srezzig looked to the others; each met his gaze with the same grim resolve. He nodded. "Deal."

Zaekshilen extended a leather-wrapped claw, surprisingly steady. Srezzig clasped it. The archivist's grip was firm, the bone-tipped claws cold against his scales. A deal, not an alliance.

"Go," Zaekshilen said, already turning back to his vials, goggles catching the first hints of dawn.

The wind shifted again, carrying the promise of morning—and the distant howl of frustrated predators.

The clutch moved out together, each wyrmling carrying their own knot of doubt, fury, and calculation. But ahead lay the hollow, the rams, and a narrow, stubborn chance—however slim—that they might still win.

They took flight, the updraft from the cliffs a treacherous ally. Zaekshilen led them not toward the open sky, but along the cliff face to another, higher ledge. There, the archivist's claws moved with feverish precision, tracing a route in chalk across the stone—a trail meant for those who didn't trust memory alone.

Srezzig studied the glowing white lines, then laid out the formation. "I take point. Ukshagg, left flank. Drozkax, you're with the archivist. Keep them in the middle."

The blue dragon took point, wings tucked tight so the wind couldn't grab them, tail flicking warning arcs around each blind corner. Ukshagg moved to his left flank, her eyes scanning constantly, recalculating risk with every shift of the cliff face. Drozkax stuck so close to Zaekshilen that the archivist's tail nearly clipped his snout, acid already bubbling hot along his gums. Hashaezkend and Shrarzeth guarded the rear, watching both the crooked trail ahead and the restless sky above.

The climb changed everything. Ledges thinned until they barely counted as ledges. The wind turned spiteful, shoving at them in unpredictable bursts. Every time a gull cried from far below, its voice hit the stone like a warning bell—too sharp, too close, too much like a predator's scream.

The path vanished, replaced by a vertical slit in the rock. Zaekshilen scaled it first, then reached down. The archivist's grip was like iron, hauling Drozkax up as if he weighed nothing. The black wyrmling grunted, surprised into silence. Zaekshilen repeated the motion for the others, a machine of unwavering strength.

As soon as Ukshagg got her foreclaws on solid ground again, she hissed upward at Zaekshilen, irritation sharpening every syllable. "What's the actual plan? You said Undragons are gathering, but you never explained why."

Zaekshilen's answer nearly vanished in the roar of the wind. "The drones you've seen—they're mindless. Hunger with wings. But when they gather in a pack... they stop being stupid. A lieutenant gives orders. And if there's a matron—" The archivist's scales shivered despite the cold. "A matron remembers being a dragon. She can think. Strategize. The more bodies there are, the more her mind stretches—like one intelligence mirrored across many mouths."

Drozkax snorted loudly, shaking grit from his frills. "Hive mind or not, they're still walking corpses. We'll melt through them."

Zaekshilen didn't bother correcting the bravado. Instead, they pulled a small vial from their pouch and held it out to him. "Keep this close. If one of them touches you—or if you touch it—use this before you taste blood. Lieutenants spread corruption fast."

Drozkax bared his teeth but took the vial. He wedged it between the scars on his shoulder where bone met membrane, as if daring anything to try him.

The ridge curved inward then, forming a shallow stone bowl slick with old lichen, its center pooled with cold shadow and unspent mist. And there—quiet, grazing, utterly unaware of the danger circling them—waited the hollow.

And the herd.

Blink rams didn't look like much—until they moved. One heartbeat they were grazing peacefully, dozens of shaggy bodies with fur the color of dry grass, heads bent low as if the world had nothing sharper than sunlight to offer. The next heartbeat, every single one vanished with a soft snap of displaced air and reappeared two body lengths away, not a single hair disturbed. Their hooves made no sound, not even on bare limestone. Their wide, glassy eyes tracked every shift in the wind like they were born knowing fear.

Ukshagg watched them for exactly six seconds before murmuring, "They're already spooked. Something's hunting from the west."

Zaekshilen nodded without looking up. "The rams always know first. When they run, you should run faster."

Srezzig glanced from the sky to the jagged rim of the bowl. "When do we move?"

Zaekshilen's claws clicked against metal as they pulled something from their pouch—a device fashioned from twisted copper wire and iridescent shell fragments that shimmered even in the weak morning light. "The Undragons will target the alpha to scatter the herd. We cripple it first. The panic will draw them in, but we control the chaos. They won't expect prey that fights back."

Hashaezkend, trembling but trying to stay focused, whispered, "What if the Undragons catch them first—"

Zaekshilen finished for her. "Then they eat until there's nothing left. And when there's nothing left, they keep eating."

Drozkax's tail cracked against the rock. "So what do you want from us? Fight them or bait them?"

Zaekshilen finally looked him in the eye, goggles gleaming. "Do what you do best. Just try not to get infected."

Srezzig spat over the edge. "We're ready. Are you?"

The archivist's smile was thin and sharp. "Always."

They crept to the rim, staying low, wings tight, steps slow. The rams blinked and twitched as one organism, herding the smallest into the center. Srezzig studied the ridgeline. At the far western edge, something flickered— like a tear opening in the air. Then a shape slid through: elongated, wrong, all claws and hunger. One Undragon. Then another. Then a third. They crawled along the cliff, jaws pried open in a silent, unnatural gape.

Ukshagg's voice barely rose above the wind. "They're waiting. Not attacking."

Zaekshilen whispered back, "They learn." Srezzig met Ukshagg's gaze. Her eyes were already fixed on the silent second Undragon, calculating its trajectory. He tossed the emitter. "The silent one. You see the angles." She caught it without a word.

The Undragons launched. The first shrieked, a metallic howl that staggered the rams. The second descended without a sound. The third scuttled forward on six limbs, a nightmare insect.

The herd stampeded. Srezzig charged the shrieking Undragon, ducking under a swipe to snap the creature's tendon with a brutal kick. It buckled, screaming a broken, jagged sound. Behind him, Hashaezkend and Shrarzeth flanked the herd, keeping them moving as one.

Ukshagg sprinted to meet the silent Undragon. She dodged its lunge, slid under its jaw, and shoved the emitter into its throat. The device detonated with a sound that folded the air on itself. The Undragon convulsed, then fled into the rocks.

Drozkax took the third. This one was bigger, slower, more rot than muscle, its limbs stiff with decay. Drozkax let it chase him, taunting it with clipped wingbeats and short, sharp feints. Then he spun, spat a stream of acid into its face, and watched it howl—clawing at its own skull, trying to rip the agony free. Drozkax darted beneath its guard, slashed open its exposed belly, then booted it over the ledge into the bowl where the rams had already fled.

Zaekshilen stayed at the rim, steady as stone. When the wounded first Undragon limped toward them, the archivist threw their net—woven with sigils, bone, and shimmering thread—directly over its skull. The creature convulsed once, then collapsed, trapped and twitching.

"Sample secured," Ukshagg called.

Srezzig swept the hollow with a quick glance. The herd was safe— already spreading across the far grass, grazing as if chaos wasn't still clawing at the cliffs behind them. His chest loosened, the tight coil behind his ribs finally going slack. He signaled the others with a flick of his tail.

It lasted less than a second.

A new shadow slid across the bowl. Enormous. Silent. It didn't scream or rush—it simply hovered, eclipsing the sun with cold, deliberate malice.

Zaekshilen's voice dropped to a whisper. "The matron."

The matron Undragon was all bone and wings, her jaw stretched into a permanent rictus. Her eyes were twin pits of oil, swallowing light. She stared at them, then at her captured brood, then at the blinking herd below.

Ukshagg's calculations fell apart mid-thought. Hashaezkend crouched low, dragging Shrarzeth close beneath her wing. Drozkax stared upward, acid gathering along his gums but frozen there, refusing to fall.

Srezzig stepped forward anyway. "We have what you want," he called, voice steady through force of will. "Leave the herd and we'll release your kin."

The matron didn't respond. Instead she descended, every bone in her body clicking into place like a lock closing. Up close, Srezzig saw the truth of her: runes carved into her chest, patches of fungus eating into her scales, old wounds split open and never healed.

Zaekshilen moved before anyone else. The archivist lifted the thrashing net with trembling claws. "We offer this," they said. "Take it and leave."

A long, ice-thin moment stretched between them.

Then the matron lowered her head. Her jaws parted just enough to taste the wounded Undragon's scent. Slowly—almost tenderly—she reached out and tore the net apart with a single swipe.

The wounded Undragon spilled free, scrambled to her side, and huddled beneath her ruined wing.

Srezzig braced for an attack—for a lunge, a roar, the inevitable fury of something that had forgotten how to die.

Instead, the matron simply looked at him. Then at Zaekshilen. Then, one by one, she fixed her oil-black gaze on every wyrmling standing frozen on the cliff.

Ukshagg whispered, barely breathing, "She's memorizing us."

Zaekshilen's reply was quiet, resigned. "They always do."

The matron lingered for one last heartbeat, as if committing every scale and scar to memory. Then she turned away. She gathered her kin beneath the tattered shadows of her wings and, with a single, thunderous beat, lifted off. The Undragons rose as one, arcing over the cliff and dissolving into the bright morning glare like smoke caught in wind.

Srezzig let out the breath he'd been crushing in his chest. "Move. Now."

They herded the rams down through the hollow—Ukshagg and Drozkax flanking the herd, Hashaezkend and Shrarzeth guiding from behind, keeping the youngest blink rams from scattering. Zaekshilen collected the torn remnants of the sigiled net, tucking each piece away before following in silence, looking strangely, almost grimly, satisfied.

At the base of the ridge, the rams blinked into the rocks and vanished—safe, for now. The clutch regrouped at the bottom, battered, bruised, but still on their feet.

Zaekshilen dusted the last streaks of chalk from their claws, then faced Srezzig. "You did better than I expected."

Srezzig bared a tired, crooked grin. "You did exactly what I thought you would."

Drozkax growled under his breath, wings twitching with leftover adrenaline. "Next time, I'm melting the matron too."

Ukshagg, exhausted beyond calculation, actually laughed. "You'll need a lot more than acid for that one."

Hashaezkend pressed close to Srezzig, tremors still running through her limbs but pride glowing in her eyes. Shrarzeth leaned in, nuzzled her neck, and whispered, "Told you we'd make it."

The sky was clear, but the clean air felt wrong. The matron's shadow was gone, but her oily gaze remained, a promise burned into his mind. She knew them now. She was remembering.

Srezzig looked at his clutch—at the new scars, the grit, the exhaustion. They hadn't won. They had survived. And they had been marked.

For now, it would have to be enough.

Chapter 8: Shadows and Scales

The world was silver and black, the ridge a knife-thin line over nothing. Srezzig's claws dug into the frost-hard stone as he scanned the valley. Beside him, the clutch held their positions. Below, blink rams grazed in twos and threes, each step precise. Every few heartbeats, one would vanish with a silent pop and reappear a body-length away—living mines, and the Undragons on the far rim were the pressure plate. Shrarzeth's eyes tracked both, her tail coiled over the drop.

Srezzig raised one foreclaw and made three crisp gestures every wyrmling knew by heart: danger—Undragons—hunting pattern. The first pair cut stark silhouettes across the valley floor, even in the peak's shadow. They prowled together, wings pinned tight, necks coiled like sprung wires. But the third—she was the real threat—clung to the eastern rockface, letting the others draw attention while she mapped every route inward. Srezzig's claws moved again: third predator, eastern wall, stealth approach.

Ukshagg read each gesture with her entire body, muscles shifting as she calculated angles and escape paths. Hashaezkend went flat, nearly invisible in the frost, wings trembling but silent. Zaekshilen's hooded expression revealed nothing—only a calm nod as they pointed: herd, patrol, tight window. Drozkax bristled openly, acid already warming behind his teeth, hatred for Undragons written across every line of his posture. And Shrarzeth—smallest but fiercest—tapped the stone twice, the silent signal for second watch: she'd track splinter patrols and any shift in wind that meant they'd been spotted.

The plan was brutally simple. Ukshagg's phantoms would distract. The rest would slip down the far side. If everything held, they'd reach the hollow before the Undragons repositioned.

Srezzig flicked a claw. Go.

Ukshagg pressed both palms to the ground, pulling frost and tension into herself. Golden light flared, splitting into three perfect copies—Srezzig, Drozkax, and, almost as an afterthought, Hashaezkend. The phantoms scattered and ran, each veering toward a different stretch of valley.

Srezzig moved next, sliding low, every muscle braced for the first sign of exposure. He committed fully—no half-measures, no hesitation—always the shield between his clutch and danger. Zaekshilen glided after him as though born to stonework. Then Shrarzeth, small, silent, and surgical, using every fissure and patch of lichen for cover. Hashaezkend and Drozkax came last. Hashaezkend flowed like smoke—present, yet not entirely. Drozkax barely contained his impatience, a bead of acid sizzling where it landed on the stone. When a pebble skittered loose, Drozkax froze beneath Srezzig's glare, molten rage swallowed by a hard lump of shame.

The valley ahead was a tangle of old rockslides and fresh snow. Blink rams grazed and blinked, coats catching the rising light like woven silver. Halfway down, Srezzig halted them. On the far side, the Undragon patrol had broken formation. Two paced the rim, heads low, wings twitching at every phantom. The third—the clever one—remained buried in shadow, eyes locked on the ridge, waiting, patient, for the real clutch to give themselves away.

Srezzig considered his options. Run and hope Ukshagg's next illusion held. Or double back and gamble on a longer, far more exposed route. He liked neither. Zaekshilen slid closer, voice barely there. "The third won't move until she's certain. If she spots you, the others collapse in."

Srezzig's reply was silent: he made himself larger, an obvious, irresistible target. Ukshagg caught the cue instantly and sent another phantom sprinting straight at the lurking Undragon. The creature snapped it out of existence in a single bite. Her posture changed in an instant—no patience now, only hunger sharpened into urgency. She launched. The other two followed as one. All three went for the rams.

Srezzig barked once—sharp command. Now.

The clutch bolted. Blink rams detonated outward in flashes of silver-blue light. The Undragons split—one barreled after the nearest cluster, while the other two swung wide to flank.

Zaekshilen murmured, "They learn from everything."

"Go left—around the hollow," Srezzig ordered.

Ukshagg and Hashaezkend veered right, phantoms flickering behind them like scattered embers. Shrarzeth darted through the shadows like a hummingbird, angling to flank the watchers. Drozkax stayed with Srezzig, snarling under his breath. Zaekshilen held his position, coiled with readiness.

They reached the hollow just as the first Undragon collided with a ram mid-teleport, jaws closing around blue fur before the blink completed. Even Drozkax froze, one hand half-raised as though he'd been about to issue an order and forgot what it was.

Ukshagg hissed, her voice tight with calculation. 'They're adapting faster than my models predicted.' Zaekshilen's grim nod was all the confirmation Srezzig needed.

Srezzig met the archivist's gaze, then glanced at Shrarzeth—who had gone rigid, reading the wind like a line of script. Ukshagg's next illusion shattered the tension: an almost-perfect blink ram, flickering in and out with uncanny precision. Two Undragons peeled away to chase it, instinct overriding strategy.

Srezzig signaled the advance. The clutch slipped through the gap, shadows hugging their backs, wind carrying their scent upward instead of out.

They passed two steaming carcasses. Drozkax slowed, eyes burning with interest.

"No time. Move," Srezzig snapped.

They reached the far edge of the hollow, breath harsh, silence pressing.

Zaekshilen perched on a jagged rock, voice steady and low. "You see it now, don't you?"

'They adapt,' Srezzig murmured, the thought coiling in his gut. Ukshagg looked at him, her amber eyes reflecting the cold dawn. 'We're not just prey. We're the next lesson.'

They prepared, bracing themselves for whatever dawn—and the Undragons—would teach them next.

A scream tore through the silence—nothing natural, nothing right. One heartbeat the hollow held only wind and the ghosts of prey. The next, it was drowning in blood and horror. Every wyrmling went rigid. Even Zaekshilen's jaw trembled.

Srezzig moved first. "Hold," he hissed, tail snapping out to flatten everyone against the ground. Above them, shadows shifted—the patrol had changed course. They weren't hunting rams anymore. They had circled back, herding something smaller. Srezzig spotted it in a crevice past the first outcrop.

A corrupted dragon. Smaller than a wyrmling, its scales buried beneath a pelt of fungus, wing membranes shredded and weeping. One eye gold. One eye black as a pit. Cornered.

The first Undragon dropped on it, pinning it down and tearing its throat open. The second ripped off a wing. The third simply watched, head cocked, its gaze fixed on the point where wing met shoulder—as if memorizing the anatomy of the kill for later study.

Drozkax went utterly still. The acid gathering in his jaws turned cold. His gums dried to dust. All that snarl, all that swagger—gone. His wings hung limp at his sides.

"They're killing their own," he breathed, voice hollow.

Ukshagg's claws scraped the dirt, tracing frantic lines. 'It's a pattern,' she whispered, her voice strained. 'They're pruning their own. The ones that don't fit... they're removed. We have to move.'

"Ukshagg—double the illusions. Ridge, now." Srezzig's voice left no room for argument.

She released a sharp pulse of energy. Behind scattered rocks, a phantom herd erupted into being—six shimmering rams in full panic, scrambling up the far slope. The Undragons froze, blood dripping from their claws. Then two launched after the decoys. The third stayed only long enough to finish the job, dragging the corpse over the ledge like discarded meat.

The clutch stayed pressed to the earth. Drozkax stared at the dying place, unable to look away from it, unable to stop himself from looking. Shrarzeth nudged him with her tail—small, steadying. Srezzig crawled closer, his voice rough but gentler than before. "We move now. They hunt weakness. Don't give them any."

Drozkax lifted his head. "They'll do it to us."

"Not if we don't let them." Srezzig rose.

Hashaezkend crept forward behind him. Ukshagg wove a thin veil of mist. Shrarzeth cast a faint shimmer over each of them, blurring their shapes like heat on stone.

"You're on point, Drozkax—get us down," Srezzig said, flicking the black wyrmling's tail.

Shrarzeth gave him a fierce nod. Drozkax shot forward in a low zigzag, not daring to look back. Ukshagg and Hashaezkend followed in tight formation. Zaekshilen and Srezzig brought up the rear. Shrarzeth stayed just ahead of Srezzig, eyes sharp, scanning every shadow.

They reached the bottom of the hollow just as the patrol doubled back—three silhouettes corralling nothing but empty air. A perfect machine. Always three. Never more.

They kept to the deepest shadows, moving as one, paws silent on stone. Half a mile out, the echoes finally faded. Drozkax slowed, voice small. "We're not like them, right?"

"Not yet," Srezzig said.

Ukshagg added quietly, "If we stick to the plan, we won't have to find out."

Hashaezkend shivered.

They pushed on beneath a sky that offered no answers. Alive. For now, that was enough.

At the hollow's edge, everything held its breath. The blink rams were jittery, their pauses between jumps stretching far too long. Drozkax paced in a tight loop, every step vibrating with barely contained fury. Hashaezkend drifted away from the group, eyes locked on a jagged outcrop. Shrarzeth followed her gaze—one patch of stone was *too* quiet.

She crept forward, slipping between the nervous rams. Wedged beneath two boulders lay a young blink ram, its leg twisted at a sickening angle, fur sparking with frantic static. It trembled so hard the stones around it rattled. The sight hit Shrarzeth like a blow—small, broken, helpless. She remembered being that tiny herself, scales still ghost-pale, the nest ledge giving way beneath her before her wings were strong enough to catch the air.

She dropped to her belly, making herself small and harmless. The ram's terrified eyes locked onto hers. 'Shrarzeth, no,' Srezzig hissed from the rocks, but the sound was distant. Her focus was absolute. She extended one claw, moving as slowly as breath, the instinct to heal overwhelming the instinct to survive.

The ram jerked, tried to blink out—but the pain pinned it in place. Hashaezkend crouched beside her; Ukshagg moved in close. Zaekshilen's voice cut across the tension, steady and unyielding: "We don't have time."

Shrarzeth didn't hear it. She lowered her snout to the ground, breathing in the sharp sting of ozone, blood, and raw fear, and murmured something soft—almost a lullaby. The ram blinked once, twice, then seemed to fold inward instead of teleporting. Its ragged breaths warmed her scales.

"Srezzig!" Ukshagg's voice carried a warning edge.

But Shrarzeth was already lifting the ram carefully, cradling it against her chest. Its breathing steadied; the rigid muscles eased. Not healed—but no longer drowning in pain.

Srezzig landed beside them. "We need to move—now."

Hashaezkend reached out. "I can take it." Shrarzeth shifted away, wings curling protectively around the trembling creature. She met Hashaezkend's eyes—kind, but immovable. The injured ram burrowed deeper into her hold, its breaths falling into rhythm with hers.

A glob of acid sizzled in the dirt beside Shrarzeth. 'You're going to get us killed,' Drozkax snarled. Srezzig met his gaze, a single sharp look that cut the protest short. Without pausing, he issued his orders. 'Ukshagg, decoys. Drozkax, our backs. Zaekshilen, with me.'

Ukshagg conjured a rush of phantom rams that scattered in every direction. The Undragons hesitated, torn—then two lunged after the illusions while one came straight for the clutch.

They bolted toward a dark cave mouth carved into the next ridge. Shrarzeth reached the entrance first, hugging the shadows, the ram tight in her claws. Hashaezkend stayed close, forming a shield around them. Drozkax held the pursuing Undragon off just long enough for Srezzig and Zaekshilen to bring it down—fangs sinking deep, acid and blood soaking into the dust.

They tumbled into the cave. Ukshagg and Hashaezkend dove in first; Shrarzeth followed with the injured ram clutched tight against her chest. Drozkax staggered in last, gasping, acid still fizzing between his teeth. Srezzig settled near the entrance, wings spreading wide to shield the clutch—and their unexpected guest—from whatever waited outside.

Shrarzeth set the ram down gently on a patch of soft moss. She closed her eyes, drew a steadying breath, then gently touched the creature's mangled leg. A soft glow radiated from her claws, and her saliva, shimmering as she licked the wound, seemed to soothe the raw flesh. Beneath the fur, bone shifted with faint clicks, sliding back into place as the ram's panicked bleating faded to soft snorts.

Outside, the patrol prowled just beyond the threshold—three dark silhouettes pacing the stone, too cautious to cross. Zaekshilen murmured, voice low enough not to echo, 'They're cautious. They won't enter another's territory without reason. It's an old predator's instinct, and right now, it's keeping us alive.'

Drozkax let out a long, shuddering breath, exhaustion and relief tangled together. "We're safe... at least for now."

Ukshagg was already calculating how many seconds of safety that really bought them. Hashaezkend leaned close, touching shoulder to shoulder with

Shrarzeth. The smaller dragon nudged the trembling ram with a quiet, instinctive tenderness—a wordless promise: *We survive. All of us.*

In the darkness, the clutch huddled close. Srezzig could feel the warmth radiating from his siblings and hear the soft, steadying breaths of the injured ram. Outside, the wind howled, a reminder of the predators that waited. But here, in this pocket of shadow, there was only the sound of them, breathing together. For now, it was enough.

Chapter 9: The Undragon Ambush

Dawn came fast and mean, no warning, no gray—just dark and then brutal light. The Windscour Cliffs stretched out white and brutal beneath an empty sky, every ledge a place you could die. The cold was vicious— needling the bone—but Srezzig wasn't thinking about that. He had eyes only for the hunt.

Five wyrmlings. Five jobs. Srezzig held the center, watching a cluster of blink rams pinned halfway up the limestone—nowhere to go but down or straight into their jaws. His clutch fanned out in a half-circle along the ridge, wings tucked tight, claws ready for whatever bolted first.

Ukshagg was already at work. The gold wyrmling's claws carved shapes into the air, and suddenly there were things that weren't quite there— shimmers, flickers, half-formed predators made of light and suggestion. They were just real enough to spook the rams toward the ledge. The illusions crackled and phased, sometimes looking like dogs, sometimes looking like fear itself. Srezzig watched two rams crash into a phantom wall and rebound straight toward the middle. Good. That was the point.

On the left, Hashaezkend flattened herself against the rock, murmuring something Srezzig couldn't quite hear. Whatever she whispered slid under the rams' skin—he saw their legs soften, their eyes go glassy. The pearl-scaled wyrmling had always been good at draining the panic out of anything living.

Shrarzeth hung back at the far edge, eyes flicking between the rams and Srezzig. She could vanish into sunlight when she wanted, turn her scales reflective enough to blind. Srezzig flicked her a signal. She leaned in and breathed out a bronze shimmer that caught the rising light, bending it into another illusory barrier. The rams shuffled closer, boxed in on all sides by things that weren't real but felt real enough.

On the perimeter, Drozkax had wedged himself behind a frost-crusted boulder and was methodically peeling scales off his own tail, examining each one and then flicking it away. Every so often he'd crane his neck to watch it tumble down the cliff face, as if that were the only thing happening worth his attention. When he caught Srezzig staring, he held up another loose scale between two claws, considered it with great seriousness, and let it go.

Everything was set.

Srezzig snapped his tail: *go time.*

Ukshagg thickened the ghost-lines. Hashaezkend's murmuring sharpened into a low pulse that made the rams flatten their ears. Shrarzeth threaded her bronze shimmer through the illusions—tiny sparks dancing in the air, pulling the herd away from the drop and deeper into the trap.

For a heartbeat, nothing moved. Even Drozkax straightened, sensing the tension twist.

The nearest ram's nostrils flared.

The herd tensed—

And Srezzig launched.

He hit the ground running, low and fast, nothing but gravity and momentum. Jaws wide, wings spread just enough to drag at the air and keep his descent controlled. The rams panicked instantly—half blinked away, the rest collided in a knot of kicking legs and tangled horns. A few popped upward in wild teleports and reappeared even worse off than before.

Srezzig caught the closest one. His teeth sank into fur and flesh—not deep, just enough to draw blood and break its focus. The ram screamed, tried to blink again, but Srezzig held tight. One down.

Ukshagg was there a second later, pinning the next three. Every time a ram vanished, her claws were waiting the instant it snapped back into existence.

Hashaezkend moved in softer. She hummed low—Srezzig felt it in his teeth—and pressed her claws against the bleeding ram's wound, slowing its pulse and steadying its fear.

Shrarzeth swept the edges, her glow dimming as she laid down one final ring of fake molten rock to seal off any escape route. The whole setup clicked into place like clockwork. Almost pretty, in a brutal way.

Then everything went to hell.

A shriek split the air above them—metallic, wrong. The sky seemed to crack open, and the Undragons poured through.

Three slammed onto the ledge at once, wings locked tight, bodies all twisted muscle and jutting bone. Leading them was a lieutenant—horns curled back and smoking at the tips, jaw stretched too wide, teeth like splintered glass. But the voice that followed was crystal clear.

"Take the wyrmlings! The master wants them alive!"

The words bypassed Srezzig's ears and punched straight into his bones. His body locked for a beat—then rage took over.

Drozkax moved first. Pure, reckless violence. He spat acid in a wide arc that caught the first attacker center mass. The thing screamed but didn't stop coming.

Ukshagg snapped up a ghost-wall between the lieutenant and the clutch. Two Undragons crashed into it and bounced off. The third punched straight through, barreling for Srezzig.

Hashaezkend crouched over the blink rams, trying to shield them. They scattered anyway—panicked blinking leaving blue-white afterimages that hung in the air like ghosts.

Shrarzeth circled behind the lieutenant, her bronze light blooming into the illusion of a collapsing ledge. The creature hesitated—only a heartbeat, but enough.

Srezzig met its charge head-on. The lieutenant hit the stone hard, claws tearing trenches. Srezzig rolled aside and grabbed for its face, but corrosive spit splashed across his shoulder. Pain ripped through him. He roared, latched onto its throat, and bit down—hard.

Drozkax tangled with two smaller Undragons. Acid and tail strikes flew everywhere. They finally overpowered him, slamming his head against the rock with a sickening crunch of scale on stone. He went limp for a second, stunned.

Ukshagg juggled ghost-walls and decoys, sending phantom Srezzigs sprinting in opposite directions. One attacker peeled off after a fake, but another lunged straight for her. She dodged—almost—but still lost the edge of her wing to raking claws.

Hashaezkend dragged two rams behind a spire of rock, trying to keep them alive as the world disintegrated.

Shrarzeth saw Drozkax pinned and unleashed a blinding bronze flare. The attackers reeled. She darted in, claws slicing, severed one tail clean through, and freed Drozkax's arm.

In half a minute, the ledge became a battlefield—blood smeared across stone, rams teleporting in panicked bursts, patches of acid smoking holes through frost. Srezzig still had the lieutenant locked in his jaws.

Then the thing laughed. Actually laughed, a sound scraped from something that remembered joy only as torment.

"Little hero," it hissed. "You taste just like your matron."

Srezzig bit down harder, felt cartilage pop. Black blood gushed, slick and reeking. The creature grinned wider.

"Incoming!" Ukshagg shouted, throwing up another wall. The last Undragon smashed through it and sent both Srezzig and the lieutenant skidding across the stone.

Both went tumbling over the edge. Srezzig heard a shriek cut short, then the sickening crunch of impact on a lower ledge. For a moment, he thought Drozkax was lost.

Everything froze.

The dust thinned. The other attackers had fled. The cliff fell eerily quiet.

Srezzig released the lieutenant's ruined throat. It staggered, swaying, somehow still upright.

Ukshagg hovered near him, bleeding but standing. "It's not over," she rasped. "There are more."

Hashaezkend crawled from behind a boulder with two terrified rams. Shrarzeth landed beside her, dragging an illusionary herd to cover their retreat.

The lieutenant straightened, eyes burning like black coals.

"Not enough," it spat.

Srezzig looked at his battered clutch. "We're not prey," he said.

A scrape of claws on stone announced Drozkax, hauling himself back onto the main ledge. He was bruised and bleeding, but wore a feral grin. "Damn right," he muttered. "We're the storm now."

For one suspended moment, the chaos simply stopped.

And the line held.

The battlefield reeked of ozone and fear, but they had won.

Then—quiet.

The blink rams stopped trembling, wide-eyed and alert. The clutch stood together, shoulder to shoulder—no one exposed, every angle covered.

Ukshagg slumped against Srezzig. "We actually did it."

"Yeah," Srezzig murmured, voice low but steady.

Drozkax tried to look unimpressed, but the pride leaked through the cracks. Hashaezkend bumped his shoulder; he flinched, then didn't pull away.

Shrarzeth padded closer, her bronze eyes softening. "Thank you," Hashaezkend whispered.

Shrarzeth flicked her tail, almost shy. "Always."

"Eat," Srezzig said, his voice raw. "We need the strength to keep moving."

It took a moment for the order to sink in. Drozkax eyed the biggest ram, the adrenaline slowly draining from his frame. Hashaezkend crouched by another, whispering a soft lament to the dying creature. Ukshagg and Srezzig remained on watch, scanning the horizon as the sky brightened.

"Why did they want us alive?" Ukshagg asked quietly.

Srezzig didn't look away from the distance. "Maybe the matron's afraid of what we're becoming."

Shrarzeth hummed, a low melodic thread. "Then let's give her something to be afraid of."

They ate together as the sun edged over the horizon, turning every scale into firelight. And for one fragile moment, the clutch felt like family again.

The first sign was the silence—so heavy and absolute that even the wind seemed to hold its breath. Srezzig had just finished the last bite of ram when something rolled through the cliff like a shockwave. Every scale on his body buzzed with the force of it. The blink rams went rigid, little sparks of static crackling through their wool.

Ukshagg's eyes went wide. "That's seismic... but it's too steady."

Hashaezkend pressed herself against Drozkax, trembling so hard her claws scraped the stone. Shrarzeth drifted closer to both of them, her bronze scales flickering as she tried to shield them with her glow.

The rumble deepened, the steady vibration climbing in pitch until it became a shriek that speared straight through bone—a sound both heard and felt. Srezzig tried to move, but the sound pinned him in place, freezing his muscles mid-breath.

Then he saw it on the horizon.

An Undragon easily ten times the size of any lieutenant, wings torn with ragged holes and rimmed in black fire. Its scales looked like shattered obsidian, each piece held together by open wounds leaking pure darkness. When it landed on the ledge, everything stopped—sound, breath, even thought.

Its exhale drifted out in a blue-black fog that burned the moss to ash. Every breath cracked the stone beneath it. When it roared, the air itself warped. The blink rams sparked violently and blinked out—some never reappearing.

Ukshagg's illusions snuffed out before they even formed, destroyed by the creature's sheer presence. Hashaezkend flattened himself behind Drozkax, too terrified to speak. Even Drozkax's usual cocky grin was gone, replaced by something tight and unfamiliar.

Shrarzeth threw up a ring of bronze light around the clutch, but the creature's eyes—white flames flickering like living frost—cut straight through it as if it were dust.

It smiled. Slow. Deliberate. The sun vanished behind its wings. Cold rushed back in a blade-sharp wave.

Ukshagg's voice was barely a breath. "We need to move—"

Srezzig opened his mouth, but nothing came out. All that old pride, every victory from the morning—it all felt meaningless now.

It knew. And on that cliff, not one of them moved to stop it.

Chapter 10: A Legacy in Stone

They broke through the rock like a shot through bone. Five wyrmlings and Zaekshilen—wings tucked, claws out—plunged from wind and light straight into the suffocating darkness of the mountain's shadow. The crevice didn't so much open as swallow them whole. Srezzig hit first, scraping scales against jagged limestone before tumbling down a ledge with the rest of the clutch in a knot of flailing limbs and panicked hissing. Drozkax came crashing in last, trailing acid and blue-black blood, the Undragon's shriek echoing right behind him.

The landing was absolute hell. Ukshagg and Hashaezkend bounced hard off the cave floor, tails whipping into their own faces, while Shrarzeth—the youngest—skidded into a shallow pool and simply stayed there, dazed, nose barely above the waterline. Srezzig, always in front, somehow managed to stay upright. Barely. He winced as his battered shoulder slammed into stone, pain lancing down his injured wing. Behind him, Drozkax sprawled like someone had dropped a spear from the sky, already twisting to check the entrance.

Everything fell silent except for their ragged, trembling breaths. No light but a pinhole far down the tunnel, shrinking second by second as the Undragon reared up outside—its silhouette filling the gap like a nightmare made of horn and teeth, its jaw unhinging with unmistakable hunger.

The roar that followed wasn't just a sound. It was a judgment. The whole cavern shuddered, dust raining down in sheets, and every wyrmling flinched and flattened against the ground. Srezzig tried to shout a warning, but his voice was swallowed by the thunder of claws tearing into stone. Drozkax bared his teeth, acid dripping off both sides of his tongue, bracing for another round even though they all knew it was hopeless.

But it wasn't the Undragon that broke through.

It was Zaekshilen—spindly, half-wrecked, but impossibly fast. They fumbled through their satchel, yanked out a crystal the size of a talon, and cracked it once against the wall. The impact lit the cavern in a pulse of blue so sharp it felt like it split the air itself.

Srezzig blinked hard, then again, waiting for his vision to settle. The space around them was far bigger than he'd realized—maybe the size of a matron's chamber, but colder. Older. Stalactites hung from the ceiling in uneven rows, close enough that a tall man would have had to duck between them. The walls, slick and wet, caught the blue flash and hurled it downward, revealing pools and spires that stretched into cavernous depths—depths that made it clear the mountain was mostly hollow. Whatever had once run through it had left and taken the warmth with it.

Zaekshilen held the crystal steady, though their claw trembled ever so slightly.

"We should be safe here," Srezzig said, but his voice frayed on the last word. He shifted to hide a wince as he flexed his bad wing. "For now," he added, the words barely a whisper.

Drozkax didn't look convinced. "We should've killed it," he muttered, just loud enough for Srezzig to catch.

"Next time, you lead," Srezzig shot back without missing a beat.

The standoff lasted maybe a breath. Then Ukshagg—who'd barely moved since they'd crashed—suddenly scrambled up the nearest wall, pressing her snout close to the stone. "There's something here," she murmured, tracing a line with one claw.

Hashaezkend limped over. "It's just rock."

Ukshagg shook her head. "No. Look." She angled her body to catch more of the crystal's glow, and the wall shifted. A network of lines surfaced beneath the stone—too regular, too deliberate to be cracks. The lines threaded into a lattice, then swirled into a spiral, then twined into something almost recognizable before collapsing back into chaos.

Srezzig stepped in, frowning. "Runes?" He hadn't seen writing like this since the old dens—back when their matron still bothered with story lessons. But this felt older. Heavier. Like it had been carved back when mountains were younger.

Ukshagg dragged her claw along the nearest mark, and for a heartbeat the line pulsed beneath her touch, as though waking up from ages of sleep. "Draconic," she whispered, almost reverently. "Very old. Maybe proto-cipher, or maybe—" She stopped, eyes flicking to Zaekshilen.

The archivist was already halfway there. Goggles pressed to their face, notebook open, claws flying as they sketched every revealed curve and sigil. "It's a warning," Zaekshilen breathed. "Or a record. Maybe both." Their claw shook with adrenaline. "No one's written this deep since the Memory Wars."

Srezzig glanced toward the tunnel mouth, where tremors from the Undragon's tantrum still shivered through the stone, then back to the glowing runes. "Can you read it?"

Ukshagg and Zaekshilen answered at the same time. "Some of it."

Shrarzeth finally dragged herself up from the pool, tail sending slow ripples across the water as she swayed upright. "Is it a map?" she asked, her voice shaky but curious.

Ukshagg shrugged. "Could be. Could also be a list of everyone who died in here. Or instructions for what to do when the next monster comes through the wall."

Drozkax snorted, acid hissing as it hit the chilly air. "Great. We're in a tomb."

Zaekshilen didn't bother looking up. "Better a tomb than a stomach," they muttered, diving right back into their frantic sketching.

Srezzig stepped back from the wall and scanned his clutch. Hashaezkend looked half-crushed but alert, eyes darting between the runes and the archivist's notes. Shrarzeth, shivering from the cold pool, instinctively began checking her own limbs for breaks, her movements small and precise even in her daze. Drozkax paced like a caged beast, unable to sit still, constantly glancing toward the narrowing entrance as if daring something to come through.

"We hold here," Srezzig decided. "We learn what we can and we rest. If it gets in, we make our stand in the dark—not out on the edge." The words sounded braver than he felt.

Ukshagg pressed her snout closer to the runes, drew in a breath, and started to speak—

then stopped.

Listening.

Srezzig heard it too—just beneath the drip of water and the distant roar, a second rhythm. Slower. Deeper. Like the mountain itself was breathing.

Zaekshilen's claws froze mid-scratch. "It's alive," they whispered, like speaking too loudly might wake whatever they were describing.

Hashaezkend shuddered. "What is?"

Ukshagg lifted her head, eyes wide with something caught between awe and terror. "The runes. The cave. I think—" Her voice faltered. "I think it's watching us."

The temperature dropped instantly. The blue crystal light seemed to swallow every shadow, but somehow the darkness thickened, pressing close, as if waiting for something—someone—to slip.

Srezzig tensed but kept his posture steady. "Let it watch," he said, flicking a warning glance at Drozkax. "We'll be ready."

Outside, the Undragon hammered its fury against the world. Inside, the ancient silence remained untouched.

The clutch gathered around Zaekshilen—even Drozkax lingered at the edge—each pretending they weren't scared. Each reading the runes in their own way. They'd lost the sky, but for now, they still had each other. And whatever secrets this cave had chosen not to forget.

The tension from the Undragon's attack lingered, but a new focus began to cut through the fear. It started with a whisper from Ukshagg, then a gasp from Zaekshilen.

Soon, both of them were crowded around the glyphs like dragons drawn to a hoard, their earlier anxieties forgotten in the thrill of discovery.

Srezzig paced the cavern's edge, his injured wing pressed tight against his side to stem the bleeding from a cracked joint. His ears stayed pricked for any sound of the Undragon forcing its way through. Drozkax prowled the opposite wall, acid tongue flicking out, leaving faint scorch marks whenever it brushed a dripping crack. Hashaezkend just sat on a ledge, staring into nothing, like her mind had stepped out of the cave entirely.

The only sounds were Zaekshilen's pen scratching, the steady drip of acid, and Ukshagg's low whisper. "Memory-binding," she murmured, tapping the central spiral. It flared blue—the light pulsing like a heartbeat after her claw left the stone. "This is the anchor. Everything else connects to it." She traced the delicate lines feeding outward, each one ending in a different knot or rune, each marking alive for a fraction of a second under her touch.

Zaekshilen dipped their pen again and copied a perfect spiral onto fresh parchment. "Mnemonic," they muttered. "Not just writing—layered memory."

"Like a blueprint for disease," Ukshagg said, pointing to a jagged rune shaped like an open wound. Even Zaekshilen flinched. "Here—'contagion.' It actually hurts to look at."

Srezzig limped closer despite his injured wing pulling tight with every step. "You really think this explains the Undragons' sickness?"

Ukshagg's eyes brightened with sharp intensity. "Not just explains—this is guidance. Instructions. How the disease is made, how it spreads, and—" she tapped a smaller spiral pulsing faintly—"how to undo it."

Zaekshilen's claws trembled with barely contained excitement. "Then this is it. Everything we need is right here."

Drozkax finally snapped. He spun around and stalked toward them, tail lashing hard enough to splash every nearby pool. "We're trapped in a cave with monsters trying to claw their way in, and you two are babbling about magical cures? We should be running, not playing scholar!"

Ukshagg didn't even spare him a glance. "Listen: it says the Undragon leader used to be like us—corrupted by false memories. If we sever that connection at the source, the body reverts. The mind resets."

Drozkax snarled, acid slicking his fangs. "Or it kills us while we mess around with glowing scribbles. You think of that?" He spat a thin stream of acid that hissed past Ukshagg's snout.

"Would you shut up?" Srezzig barked, rubbing a fresh bruise blooming across his hip. "We're already here. If there's even a chance—"

Zaekshilen lifted one claw. "We need a distraction. This triangular rune—'resonance.' If we create enough… disruption, the protective memories will shatter."

Drozkax and Srezzig traded a look as another Undragon roar rattled the cavern walls. Finally, Srezzig exhaled through his teeth and nodded. "Fine. We try it. But if we die, I'm haunting both of you."

"Fair enough," Zaekshilen said with a crooked grin, already bent over their notes again.

Ukshagg dragged her claw over the first spiral, watching it pulse brighter, almost eager. "We move fast. Hit the core, then collapse the rest before it rebinds."

The cave fell into a breathless hush—every drip of acid, every scratch of pen suddenly too loud. Then, from the far edge of the chamber, a soft glow started to bloom, curling outward like a heartbeat made of light.

A slender figure emerged—Shrarzeth, the clan healer, her scales edged with a soft, pale glow. She placed one gentle claw on Ukshagg's torn wing and another on Drozkax's acid-scorched flank. Cool light rippled from her touch, knitting torn flesh, soothing burns, smoothing every ragged edge. Srezzig's limp eased as she hummed a low, resonant chant, and even Zaekshilen's raw, ink-stained fingertips brightened as the pain melted away.

When she finished, the wounds were gone—scales gleaming fresh, blood clotted clean, bodies restored. But Shrarzeth's own hide, once bright as moonlit water, had dulled to a brittle gray. She swayed as she backed into the darkness, her tail dragging where it once glided effortlessly. She managed a small nod—brief, determined, and costly—before collapsing deeper into the shadows, leaving the others whole while she trembled out of sight.

Ukshagg tested her wings, feathers of light shimmering off the healed membrane. "Ready."

Zaekshilen smoothed their smudged notes with steadying claws. "Then let's do this."

Srezzig braced himself at the cave entrance, watching the runes flicker with renewed fire along the walls. "Time to finish it."

Behind him, Drozkax drew in a long breath, tail-tip twitching like a blade measuring distance. The cave seemed to inhale with them—every shadow waiting, every echo holding its breath—as the clutch prepared to make their move.

The air, already thin, grew tight with unspoken arguments. Drozkax paced, his claws scraping a rhythm of pure impatience against the stone.

"This is a tomb," he snarled, finally stopping to face Srezzig. "You think these scribbles will save us? We should be fighting."

Srezzig met his gaze, too tired for another clash. "And die in the tunnel? What's your plan?"

Before Drozkax could retort, Shrarzeth spoke, her voice soft but cutting through the anger. "They're still dragons," she insisted, looking at the wall of runes. "Underneath it all. If there's a chance to save them, we have to try."

Drozkax scoffed, but the fury in his eyes faltered. He lashed his tail, scorching a new line into the stone, and fell silent. The argument was over, not settled, but postponed by a question none of them could answer.

Ukshagg and Zaekshilen bent over the runes again, their voices rising and falling in a strange, unified rhythm.

"Breaking the core should reset the mind," Ukshagg said, pointing to a fresh sketch. "Problem is getting close enough."

Zaekshilen traced the spiral pattern, then gestured at the deep cracks webbing the wall. "There's a resonance here. If we match it, the Undragon might freeze. Only for a moment, but it could be enough."

Hashaezkend drifted closer. "And then?"

Ukshagg shrugged. "Then we wing it."

Shrarzeth settled near Srezzig. "Thank you," she murmured. "For listening."

Srezzig didn't answer. He was listening—just not to her. He listened for the next roar, the next tremor in the stone, the next shift in the dark outside.

Drozkax kept pacing, circling the group like a caged thing.

The argument didn't end; it settled into the stone, a low hum of resentment beneath the scholars' whispers. The only movement was the flicker of crystal light on the walls. When the silence became heavier than any roar, Srezzig clapped his wings together. The sound cracked through the cavern.

"Enough," he said. "We rest. Tomorrow we decide."

No one wanted to sleep first, but exhaustion beat pride.

Ukshagg curled beside the runes, chin resting on her forearms, staring at the spiral until her eyes finally drifted shut. Zaekshilen hunched over the notebook, claw still scratching even as sleep overtook them. Hashaezkend found a spot by the shallowest pool and passed out instantly. Shrarzeth waited until Srezzig settled, then crept closer, her breathing gradually falling into sync with his. Even Drozkax eventually slumped against the far wall—one eye half-open, suspicious as ever, but breathing slow and deep.

Srezzig stayed awake the longest.

Keeping watch. Counting sounds—every drip of water, every tremor beyond the cave walls. He had given orders, kept his voice steady, moved them forward. But crouched here in the dark, listening to their breathing slow into sleep, he could not remember what any of that had been for.

The cave held that particular quiet that only arrives after something terrible. No one was happy. No one was safe.

But they'd made it through the night.

For now, that had to be enough.

When the fighting finally died down, Hashaezkend slipped away.

She found a crack in the wall—barely wide enough for two tails—and squeezed through, leaving the others with their anger, their plans, and their brittle pride. The side chamber was nothing special: more wet stone, a thin trickle of water, and a stale, rotting smell that clung to the air like old breath. Hashaezkend dropped in a small heap and curled as tight as she could, wings wrapped around herself like a burial shroud, claws pressed hard against her snout. The air tasted of cave fungus—sickly sweet at first, then bitter as it settled in the back of her throat.

The empathy hurt worse than any wound.

It rolled through her in unrelenting waves, filling her chest until it felt like she was drowning from the inside out. Drozkax's rage burned through her—hot, blistered, and sharp. Srezzig's bravado was a hollow ache beneath the surface, a brittle shell around something much more fragile. Ukshagg and Zaekshilen radiated obsessive tension as they scrawled and muttered over the runes, their minds wired tight as steel. And Shrarzeth—against all logic—still flickered with stubborn hope, bright as a spark refusing to die.

Hashaezkend pressed her head down and tried to shut it all out.

It didn't work.

When sleep finally came, it wasn't kind.

It began as a blur: blood on her tongue, claws scraping stone, prey-panic tangled with hunter-hunger until neither made sense—just one gnawing, endless need. Then the dream twisted, dragging Hashaezkend up and out of the cavern into cold blue air and impossible distances.

She was flying.

But not as herself. The body wasn't right—lighter, smaller, wrapped in fur instead of scales, hooves instead of claws. She looked down and saw a blink ram sprinting along a knife-edge ridge, every muscle taut, every step a wager with death. The world below was nothing but storm and shadow, a swirling pit of teeth and howling wind. Still, the ram kept running.

Something chased it. A shadow. A hunger. A half-remembered nightmare.

It howled, and the sound was every wyrmling's fear made real—a promise of extinction whispered in a voice older than dragons.

The ram didn't slow.

It leapt. The air caught it, spun it, flung it across the chasm. Instead of falling, it vanished in a burst of white-blue light. No pain. No terror. Just movement—clean and pure.

Hashaezkend watched it reappear on another ledge, whole and unbroken. The horns atop its head glowed with a soft, impossible radiance. It lowered them toward the darkness, and the shadow hesitated—confused, almost afraid.

Then another ram blinked in beside it.

Then a third.

Then more.

Each pulse of light brightened the air until the whole ridge became a shield.

The shadow hated the light. It tried to smother it, but every time it drew close, the rams flickered out and back again—always one step ahead, always moving together. Hashaezkend felt the pattern beneath their dance: a rhythm, a logic, an ancient choreography older than pain itself.

Then the vision changed.

The blink rams stood at the edge of the world, horns locked together, their combined light so bright it burned the shadows straight out of the sky. An Undragon—massive, ruined, hollow to its core—clawed its way up the cliff's edge. It bellowed, and the sound tore the earth in two, but the rams didn't break. They held.

One stepped forward—horn blazing—and touched the Undragon's forehead.

Where the horn met flesh, the darkness recoiled. Not completely, not forever—but enough to reveal the faint outline of something that might once have been a dragon. A face surfaced inside the shadow, terrified but unmistakably alive.

Hashaezkend tried to shout, to warn someone—anyone—but the dream thickened, warped, then shattered. The vision collapsed into chaos: spinning runes, screaming wind, the sharp taste of blood and ozone. And at the center of it all, a single phrase whispered in a dozen overlapping voices:

"The essence binds the memory. The horn carries the cure."

She jolted awake, gasping, mouth full of stone dust, limbs tangled in her own wings. It took her a second to remember the cave. Another to realize she wasn't alone.

Srezzig crouched just inside the crack, blocking the only exit, eyes full of questions he hadn't dared ask aloud. Shrarzeth hovered over his shoulder, scales glowing with equal parts hope and worry. Ukshagg and Zaekshilen stood farther back, holding up the blue crystal like a lantern, both of them pretending not to care while very clearly caring. Even Drozkax lurked in the shadows, doing his best impression of someone bored out of his mind—and failing spectacularly.

Hashaezkend pushed herself upright, but the world listed sideways. Srezzig caught her, steadying her with one wing.

"You were screaming," he said, voice rough but gentle.

Hashaezkend tried to laugh; it came out thin, more cough than amusement. "Just a dream."

Shrarzeth inched closer, tail coiled tight enough it trembled. "What did you see?"

Hashaezkend searched for words and found only fragments. "The rams. The light. They can fix this. Not just run from it." She turned toward Ukshagg and Zaekshilen, pulse skittering. "The runes say the same thing, don't they? That the energy can break the curse—if it gets close enough?"

Ukshagg blinked, then nodded slowly. "The resonance is literal, then. Not just a concept. But..."

She glanced at Zaekshilen, who had already begun scribbling like a creature possessed.

"The horn carries the cure," Zaekshilen muttered. "Of course. Of course."

Drozkax grumbled but didn't stalk off. "So what—you want us to grab a ram and throw it at the monster?"

"Something like that," Srezzig said dryly. "But we do it together."

For the first time, real hope shivered through Hashaezkend's chest—dangerous, blinding hope.

"I know how to help them," she whispered. "The blink rams aren't just prey. They're the cure."

The words hung in the chamber, bright enough to make even Drozkax go still.

For a long moment, no one spoke. Every wyrmling was already seeing the impossible plan unfolding in their heads. Sable looked around at their faces and found no fear there—only the particular stillness that came just before they did something stupid.

Srezzig smiled—tired, battered, but fierce. "We finish this tomorrow."

Hashaezkend nodded, already imagining how to shepherd light through darkness.

Outside, on the ridge above them, the first pale hints of dawn began pushing back the night.

Chapter 11: The Horde Descends

Srezzig stepped out of the cave first, his clutchmates tight behind him. Their claws hit frost-covered stone, each step cracking through the morning's ice with sharp, brittle sounds. Windscour Ridge spread out to the east, but here in the ravine everything felt close—ledges like knife edges, air thick with waiting. When Srezzig spread his wings for balance, his old injury flared hot. He folded them back quick. No point showing weakness.

The sun wasn't up yet, but the sky had already gone pale. Light caught the far slope, and it glittered—not with dew. Too many scales.

Ukshagg went still, scanning the horizon, then the ravine wall. Every gold fleck on her hide seemed to harden. Srezzig followed her stare and his stomach dropped.

Undragons. Not a patrol—a living avalanche of them. Bodies stacked on bodies, heads bristling with jagged horn, so many he couldn't count, layered in the mist. They clung to the vertical rock face like insects. They filled the narrow choke of the ravine below. Then the smell hit him—rot, static, and the cold iron tang of blood not yet spilled. It coated his mouth, a taste like biting down on a live coal.

Behind him, the clutch froze.

Zaekshilen stumbled out of the dark, clutching their satchel, goggles smeared, face caught between calculation and panic. Their claws shook as they checked the vials, then the notebook, then the battered gold-scale samples. Drozkax came next, wings spread, tongue already working up acid, but his bravado was thin. Every movement screamed alarm.

Hashaezkend brought up the rear, half-dragging a blink ram. Its legs twitched, blue-white fur crusted with dried blood. The ram shivered but made no sound. The pearl wyrmling held it close, like a living shield.

Srezzig spat. "They're blocking every exit."

"They found us," Ukshagg whispered, voice barely holding. Her claws were already pulling energy from the rock, weaving the first threads of illusion—the only weapon they had left.

Zaekshilen started shaking, fear drowning out even their hunger for knowledge. "This is—" They couldn't finish.

Srezzig locked eyes with them. "No time. Form up, defensive, now!"

Ukshagg's voice cracked like lightning on stone. "Won't work. They've sealed both ends." Her eyes darted, mapping invisible paths, then her pupils shrank to pinpoints. "Every way out is..." She swallowed hard, throat scales rippling. "We're trapped."

Drozkax hissed at the nearest Undragon and spat a warning arc of acid onto the ground. It sizzled against cold stone, filled the air with chemical bite.

The enemy didn't care. They advanced with a kind of broken, hungry logic. Some crawled upside-down, belly to the wall, claws gripping where nothing should hold. Others bounded in the open, using rock as a springboard, landing with wet thuds and sick grins. Nothing elegant about them. Every movement a challenge, every scar a history of eating rivals.

Srezzig's claws flexed against stone, his body coiling to spring before his mind caught up. The matron's training dissolved into useless fragments— theory that meant nothing now. His scales tingled with pure instinct, primal knowledge singing in his blood: they'd die here unless someone—him—tore through that line.

"Ukshagg! Phantoms, everywhere!" he roared. "Hashaezkend, Shrarzeth, keep the blink ram alive. Drozkax—"

"Ready," Drozkax lied, wings flared wide.

Zaekshilen's voice came back, shaky but determined. "We can use the ledge. They won't risk collapse with the matron watching." They pointed past the layered ranks to the far wall where a shadow loomed. At first Srezzig thought it was a trick of light. Then the shadow moved.

The leader.

Three times the height of the others, stitched together from the worst mutations: wings longer than a cart's span, tail lashed with spines, face armored with horn and fungus. The eyes were wrong—glowing blue fire but also empty, like the skull behind them had already died. Even the front ranks edged away, a ripple of terror spreading through the horde.

For a second, Srezzig dared to hope that fear could be turned. "If we can reach the wall, use the blink ram, maybe—"

Ukshagg shook her head. "There's no path. They'll close every gap."

"Then we make one," Srezzig spat.

The Undragons shrieked as one, a wave of sound that rippled across rock. They started to run—not a charge but a coordinated bleed, bodies swarming around every obstacle, every curve, every bad handhold.

Ukshagg unleashed the illusions, filling the field with a storm of false wyrmlings, each perfect for a split second then gone. It worked—some Undragons went for the bait, jaws snapping on nothing—but there were too many. The real clutch was still exposed.

Zaekshilen ducked low, pressed tight to Srezzig's flank. "If we die, burn the notebook," the archivist whispered, words so fast he almost missed them. "Don't let them remember."

Srezzig didn't answer. Whatever plan there'd been was gone. Only reaction left.

The front Undragons reached the ledge base, claws scraping sparks. The line shivered, then went liquid. Srezzig counted three, five, eight bodies jostling to be first, each one hissing, spitting, snapping at air.

"On my mark," Srezzig said. "We go up and over."

Drozkax bared his teeth. "We'll never outrun them."

"Doesn't matter. We don't let them choose where we die."

Shrarzeth made a soft sound. "The blink ram. It wants to run."

Srezzig nodded. "Then let it."

Ukshagg prepped the last illusions, face tight with effort, sweat beading between her scales.

Then the signal.

Srezzig went first, launching off the narrow ledge, his bad wing burning with every beat. Drozkax right behind, using acid to keep the ledge slick, making every enemy step misery. Ukshagg and Hashaezkend followed, the blink ram held tight between Shrarzeth's claws, eyes wide with wild light.

The Undragons snapped at their heels, but Ukshagg's illusions flickered and split, leaving them biting ghosts. The climb was pure terror—claws slipped, wings caught on rock—but desperation made them fast, made them reckless.

Halfway up, the wall shook. The matron roared, and the front ranks hesitated. Just a heartbeat. But enough.

Srezzig reached the top, flung himself over, then turned to haul Ukshagg up. She nearly slipped but his grip held. Hashaezkend scrambled after. Shrarzeth followed with the blink ram. Drozkax fended off the closest pursuers with acid that caught the nearest Undragon full in the face.

They ran. The ridge narrowed, forcing them close, every step risking a fall. Behind them the horde poured after, the leader's eyes fixed on them, blue fire washing the stones.

No plan. Only motion.

Srezzig tasted blood. Didn't know if it was his own.

The day had just begun, but the clutch was already out of time.

At the top of the world, the only way forward was down.

The ridge fell away beneath them—a jagged cut in the earth spilling dust and impossible choices. They ran because slowing down meant dying.

Ukshagg kept throwing illusions, but each one cost her. The color drained from her scales with every casting, her movements growing shakier, less solid. Her first wave scattered phantom wyrmlings across the slope—ghost bodies flickering between boulders, luring Undragons into dead ends and over cliffs. The second was smarter: fake shadows slipping into cracks, cave mouths appearing just long enough to fool the enemy before vanishing.

When Srezzig gave the signal, they cut left toward a gap in the rock barely wide enough to squeeze through. He shoved Drozkax in first, then Hashaezkend with the ram. Ukshagg stumbled through next, sweat pouring off her. Srezzig came last, spreading his wings to block as much of the opening as he could. Behind them: claws scraping stone, bodies slamming into fake caves, the frustrated snarls of enemies realizing their prey was smarter than expected.

Then Zaekshilen screamed—a sound that didn't belong in daylight.

Srezzig spun around. The archivist had gone down just above the chokepoint where old moss made the slope slick. Their satchel had flown open, notebook and vials tumbling downhill. A crystal cylinder caught the sun for one bright moment before shattering against rock.

Zaekshilen dove for the pieces like they could still be saved. "The research!" The words came out broken and desperate.

An Undragon dropped from above and pinned them with one casual swipe. Its jaw unhinged, ready to tear into Zaekshilen's throat.

Everything in Srezzig went tight and electric. Could he go back? Help them and still protect the others? There wasn't time to think it through. His body decided for him.

"Ukshagg! Cover!"

Half-dead from the last spell, Ukshagg somehow pulled together one more phantom—imperfect but enough. The Undragon's head snapped toward the illusion, buying Zaekshilen a second to scramble free. They grabbed the satchel, crammed the notebook inside, and threw themselves toward the nearest crack.

Srezzig reached for them but another Undragon landed between them, claws gouging trenches in the ground. This one was bigger, older, eyes clouded white, but it moved with brutal accuracy. Srezzig's warning snarl didn't even register.

Zaekshilen looked back, face smeared with blood, goggles cracked. "Go! I'll find another way!"

Srezzig didn't want to obey. But he did.

They squeezed into the narrow passage, rock scraping scales, darkness offering brief protection. Shrarzeth's ram thrashed in panic, trying to blink away but too stressed, too trapped. The pearl wyrmling held it close, whispering meaningless comfort just to keep it from falling apart completely.

The shrieks behind them multiplied. Ukshagg paused just long enough to smear a streak of gold blood across the wall before forcing herself through. She didn't look back.

On the other side, the terrain opened into a tilted basin of broken stone and shallow pools. Drozkax was already there, acid burns marking every approach, eyes hunting for threats. Srezzig counted heads: one, two, three. Where was Zaekshilen?

A heavy thud answered him. The archivist slammed down from above, wings beating frantically, claws barely catching the ledge. The satchel swung wild—nearly lost—but Zaekshilen caught it in their teeth and dropped to all fours, eyes huge and frantic.

Three smaller Undragons followed. Ukshagg was ready. She sent a phantom wyrmling charging at them and the group split—two chasing the fake, one bearing down on the real thing.

Drozkax seized the moment. He lunged, locked the Undragon in a chokehold, then dragged acid down its spine. The creature screamed and bucked, but the black wyrmling held on, jaws clamped, eyes burning with pure rage.

Shrarzeth shielded the ram. Srezzig moved to help but Ukshagg pulled him back. "Too many. They're trying to separate us—don't let them."

Drozkax finished it with a vicious twist and hurled the body downslope. But more Undragons were already scaling the walls, jaws gaping, tongues hanging loose.

Zaekshilen hauled themselves upright, goggles caked in blood. "I've got the notes," they rasped, "but the sample's gone. The cure—" They couldn't finish.

Srezzig shoved the archivist toward the others. "Stay close. Don't stop."

All five of them bolted into the next passage. The Undragons followed but the tunnel curved, dropped, twisted so sharply the horde had to crawl single-file. Srezzig led despite his useless wing, legs driving hard. He could hear Drozkax behind him, then Ukshagg, then Shrarzeth, then Hashaezkend still murmuring to the ram.

Zaekshilen stumbled, their legs giving out. As Srezzig turned, the archivist slammed their body against the passage walls, wings flaring to block the path. Blood-streaked scales caught the dim light as they met his gaze for a final, terrible second. Their claws dug deep for leverage, satchel tucked protectively under one foreleg.

"Go!" Zaekshilen's voice cracked as the first Undragon hit them. The impact rippled through their whole body, but they held, every muscle straining as they bit down on corrupted flesh.

Srezzig wanted to stay and fight. But Ukshagg was right—numbers would win. He ran, pulling the others with him.

Behind them, Zaekshilen's roar turned wet and choked. Claws on stone. Tearing wings. Notebook pages catching the updraft, white against the dark, scattering.

Srezzig didn't look back. Not this time.

They burst into daylight—battered, bleeding, half a clutch and one archivist who wouldn't make it out. The sky was impossibly blue for a moment, bright enough to hurt.

Then the Undragons howled, and everything went red.

The Undragons came fast—all hunger and hate, teeth snapping at the last threads of hope. Srezzig, blood on his lips, tried counting the bodies pouring down the slope. He lost track at twenty. Then fifty. Then it didn't matter anymore.

Shrarzeth clutched the blink ram close, both of them pressed flat against the rock beside Hashaezkend. Ukshagg, drenched in silver sweat, jaw locked tight, poured what was left of her magic into a storm of illusions—ghost wyrmlings spinning through the air, each one buying them another precious second. It worked, barely. But each phantom flickered weaker than the last, and the enemy was catching on. Two Undragons chased the fakes, but three more circled wide, eyes locked on the real targets.

Drozkax didn't wait for the end to come to him.

He launched forward like a black comet, claws ripping through the first Undragon in his path. His acid breath sprayed wide, splashing across three heads at once, melting flesh and scale and horn together. The creatures shrieked and stumbled back, buying Srezzig and the others a single breath of space.

"I'll hold them!" Drozkax roared, every muscle burning with rage, scales glowing in the firelight of his own destruction.

Srezzig reached for him, tried to shout something, but Drozkax was already gone—swallowed by the crush of bodies. The black wyrmling fought like he was born for it, jaws snapping, tail whipping, wings battering anything that got close. Acid poured from his mouth in streams, burning through enemies and stone alike.

For one impossible second, Srezzig thought Drozkax might actually pull it off.

Then the horde adjusted. They stopped charging him head-on, started circling instead, jaws snapping in rhythm, waiting for the acid to run out.

"Drozkax, fall back!" Srezzig screamed, but his voice was nothing against the chaos.

Ukshagg's claws trembled as she conjured one last phantom—bigger this time, meaner, a perfect copy of Drozkax. The enemy lunged for it, and for half a heartbeat, the real Drozkax broke free, wings shredded but still beating.

Hashaezkend, curled around the blink ram, whispered, "Come back." But only the wind heard.

Srezzig saw what was coming, and he hated it. There was no saving Drozkax. Not without losing everyone else. He spat blood, set his jaw, and turned to Ukshagg and Hashaezkend.

"We run," he said. The words felt like murder.

Ukshagg stared at him, not understanding. "But—"

"There's no time," Srezzig snapped, grabbing her by the scruff. "We stay, we die here."

Hashaezkend stood slowly, cradling the blink ram, eyes fixed on the black blur in the swarm. "We can't just leave him," she said, but Srezzig was already moving.

He shoved Ukshagg toward the edge. Shrarzeth and Hashaezkend followed. The only way out was a steep cascade of loose rock. It would break bones, maybe wings, but it was another minute of life.

As they scrambled, Hashaezkend looked back. Just once.

Drozkax was a storm in the center of it all, every limb a weapon, every wound a mark of defiance. But even he couldn't fight forever. The acid sputtered, then stopped. The Undragons closed in, each bite calculated to wound, not kill. They wanted him alive.

Drozkax realized it then. The truth of the trap.

For the first time, fear broke through the fury. His eyes went wide as the circle tightened.

The last thing Hashaezkend saw was the look on his face—not aimed at the enemy, but at them. At Srezzig.

Then the slope gave way beneath her, and everything blurred.

The four of them tumbled down in a tangle of blood and dust. The blink ram squirmed, nearly slipped free, but Hashaezkend held on, sobbing without sound.

Ukshagg checked their injuries, catalogued the damage, but couldn't speak. Her hands flexed once, then went limp.

Srezzig stared up at the ridge, waiting for Drozkax to appear one last time, to make that final desperate sprint, to somehow be the hero.

But only the enemy crested the edge. Dozens of them. Jaws painted with fresh black blood.

Srezzig wanted to scream, but nothing came out.

They ran—into the next canyon, into the unknown, into whatever waited for those who abandoned the line.

Above, the Undragon matron watched, the blue fire of her eyes the only mercy left in the world.

The mountain swallowed them whole. One moment they were running, the next they were nothing but instinct and terror—limbs shredded, hearts clenching and releasing like fists in their chests Every step forward was a refusal to give up. Srezzig didn't lead so much as flee, driven by pure animal need to put distance between himself and that sound behind them. He squeezed through gaps barely wide enough, threw himself around impossible turns using claw and wing, focused on nothing but the burning pain in his torn membrane. The slope dropped away beneath them, twisting into chaos. Every footfall was a prayer.

Ukshagg stumbled after him, magic gone. Her claws scraped and slipped on broken stone, fighting for any grip they could find. But even exhausted, even falling apart, her eyes kept moving—searching every outcrop and shadow for something, anything, even as everything inside her screamed to just stop.

Behind them, Shrarzeth held the blink ram against her chest, both of them shaking. The creature had given up struggling. Its fear was so complete it had gone still, and she understood that feeling perfectly. Hashaezkend walked beside them, whispering nonsense in a soft singsong—the only gentle sound left in the world.

The horde never stopped. Claws on stone, screams that didn't sound like anything living should make, the mountain itself groaning like it might split open. Ice cracking, rocks shattering, the whole world begging for it to end.

Finally they found a ledge—barely wide enough for three of them standing side by side, a straight drop on one side, the ridge above them crawling with moving shadows. Srezzig's chest heaved, each breath like swallowing knives. Beyond them, the Windscour Cliffs. Closer now, but still impossibly far.

Ukshagg collapsed, sprawled out flat. "No sign of Zaekshilen," she managed, voice like gravel.

Srezzig's wings sagged. His scales looked dull, lifeless. "We can't go back," he said, and his voice broke on the last word. His claws scraped four deep gouges in the stone—reaching for hope that wasn't there.

Shrarzeth sank down beside them, wrapping her wings around the ram. "We left them," she said quietly. That hurt worse than anything else.

Ukshagg pushed herself up one more time. "We're alive. That's something."

The silence after that was worse than the noise. They listened—for footsteps, for voices, for anything—but the mountain gave them nothing.

Shrarzeth placed her talons over the worst of their wounds. Pale green light spilled from her claws as torn flesh closed, blood stopped flowing, pain faded to something bearable. She kept going until she'd done what she could.

Srezzig looked at the four of them and the ram—all that was left. He wanted to say something that mattered, something brave. Nothing came.

"Rest," he said finally. "We move again at dusk."

No one argued. Ukshagg's breathing slowed. Hashaezkend curled up next to the ram, her tears long since dried up. Srezzig stared at the sky and counted the hours until they'd have to climb again, knowing none of them would ever be the same.

They watched the light die, wondering if the horde would find them before morning came.

Chapter 12: Broken Wings and Shattered Dreams

The impact rattled every tooth in Srezzig's skull. One heartbeat he'd been above it all—sky, wind, hunger, the hunters' nets still close enough to taste—and the next he slammed into the ravine like someone had ripped the ground up to meet him. He bounced twice and wedged onto a narrow ledge, barely stopping before the cliff could finish him. The rest of the clutch tumbled after in a mess of claws and scattering stone, each carving their own violent descent down the fractured slope. The Windscour Cliffs had never felt more like a cage.

Srezzig tried to stand. His left wing refused to move. The pain was bad—sharp, wrong—but worse was the sound: a wet, ragged drip of blood hitting shale in slow, syrupy drops. Blue—painfully blue against bone-white stone. He hissed, and the echo hissed right back, mocking him.

Ukshagg landed two lengths below, vanishing into a cloud of dust before slamming belly-first onto a shelf. Her gold scales scraped stone like she still expected something soft to catch her. She barely moved after that, just flexed one claw, then the other—checking what still worked. Blood streaked her nose, but she didn't bother wiping it. Her gaze drifted somewhere distant, brain running angles and routes and probabilities—until that collapsed, too. She tried to spark an illusion, just a flicker, but the shimmer died the moment it left her claw.

Hashaezkend was the only one who landed quietly. The pearl wyrmling hit, bounced, and then simply... stopped. Went limp, like she'd surrendered to gravity itself. A breath later her head whipped up, eyes wide and hollow, scanning for the others. When she spotted Srezzig, relief broke over her face—only to twist instantly into fresh terror, like surviving meant new ways to fail. She crawled toward Ukshagg rather than the wall where it was safer and touched those gold scales with trembling claws. Then she lifted her head, like she needed permission to keep breathing.

Shrarzeth hit last. Came down at an angle, clipped the wall, and crumpled against a boulder in a heap of bent limbs. One leg was wrong— twisted, half-crushed—blood soaking her belly and matting every scale it touched. For a heartbeat Srezzig thought she was gone. Then her chest lifted, slow and stubborn, like her body refused to die even if her spirit might've tried.

Silence fell over them—thick, heavy. Even the wind that had chased them for miles seemed to forget how to howl down here. The walls rose sharp and vertical on every side, boxing them in. A perfect trap. Also, for now, the only barrier between them and the endless teeth waiting above.

Srezzig braced against the rock and forced himself upright. His useless wing hung from him like dead weight, every shift sending jagged lightning through his ribs, but he refused to be the first to fold. He took in the clutch: Ukshagg—alive, if drifting. Hashaezkend—moving, barely. Shrarzeth—hurt, but breathing. For one fragile moment, he let himself imagine they might still get out of this together.

Then the guilt slammed into him. If he'd chosen a different ridge, fought harder, thought quicker—maybe Zaekshilen would still be here, not lost somewhere in the chaos of that desperate scramble through the peaks.

Ukshagg finally pushed herself upright, propping on two shaky legs, tail limp behind her. "We're pinned," she said, the arrogance stripped completely from her voice. "No way out. Both ends blocked. Walls too steep to climb for at least a quarter mile."

Hashaezkend tried to offer comfort—a nuzzle, a wing, anything—but her own limbs shook too violently. Instead she shifted closer to Srezzig, like being near him might somehow keep the world from collapsing.

Shrarzeth groaned—low, rough, and raw—and every head snapped toward her. She tried to push herself upright, but the leg refused, folding beneath her like wet parchment. Her claws sparked with faint green light as she tried to coax healing into the break, but the glow sputtered out like a dying candle. "I'm stuck," she whispered, barely loud enough to reach them.

Srezzig limped over, shoving his own pain somewhere far and unreachable. He examined the leg—broken, yes, but not beyond saving. Then he met her eyes, bracing for panic. Instead he found something worse: a dull, heavy acceptance, like she'd already decided what came next. That look made him want to bite straight through the cliff face.

"We'll set it," he said. "Just don't move."

Ukshagg crawled in close, claws trembling as she tried to brace the limb. Srezzig nudged her aside with a shoulder—gentle but firm—then wrapped his claws around the bone. One sharp jerk, grinding and cracking, and Shrarzeth's scream ripped through the ravine, bouncing off every wall until it felt too big for their bodies to contain.

He wrapped the break with a strip of shed scale peeled from his own side. Crude, ugly work, but it would hold. It had to.

When he finished, he slumped to the ground, his ruined wing hanging at that awful angle. Then the exhaustion found him—not a crash, but a slow, rising tide until every bone felt packed with wet sand.

For a long while, no one spoke.

Ukshagg traced patterns in the dust, trying to logic her way toward an escape, but every line she drew fell apart halfway through. Hashaezkend drifted between them, sometimes touching a shoulder, sometimes just radiating empathy so raw it made Srezzig's scales itch. Shrarzeth closed her eyes, breath thin and uneven.

Srezzig let the quiet settle around them. For the first time, he didn't try to lead or plan or pretend to hope. He just breathed. Waited for whatever came next.

It didn't take long.

Night in the ravine didn't fall—it crept in. The last thread of warmth bled out with the sun, replaced by a cold so deep it settled beneath their scales. Srezzig tried to push it aside, focusing instead on Shrarzeth's leg. The limb was already swelling, dried blood crusted dark across her bronze belly. He spotted frost-moss clinging to a crack in the rock, scraped it free, and packed it gently around the wound. Maybe the cold would help. Maybe it wouldn't.

Shrarzeth kept her teeth clenched through it all, eyes fixed on the ragged strip of sky above. "Could be worse," she muttered. "Could've lost the tail."

Srezzig huffed a short laugh. "You need that tail to keep up with us."

"Wouldn't want to slow you down, Srezzig," she shot back—sharp, but quiet.

The banter died quickly. Srezzig finished securing the wrap, then helped her drag the injured leg closer to their fireless camp—a patch of dirt framed by a half-circle of clutchmates, all pretending to rest.

Ukshagg sat farthest from the wall, staring up at the stars. Every few seconds, her head tilted as she calculated angles or distances only she could see, then she shook it off with a frustrated hiss. Up here the stars looked close enough to grab, but all she ever found was rock and disappointment.

Hashaezkend hadn't moved except to shiver. Her earlier tears had dried, but now and then a fresh one would cut a pale line down her cheek before disappearing into the dirt. She huddled between Srezzig and Shrarzeth, wings pulled tight, body trembling with everything she refused to voice. It would've been easier if she'd screamed or struck the stone. Instead she just sat there, absorbing everyone else's hurt and making it heavier.

Srezzig's stomach cramped with hunger. He watched Ukshagg spot a beetle crawling across the wall—one quick flick of her tongue, and she caught it, chewing slowly, savoring the tiny shot of protein. He found himself staring—not judging, just envious.

"Forward is death," Shrarzeth whispered, a thread of dark humor bleeding through. "We're trapped. Stay here, we starve. Run, we get torn apart."

"We rest," Srezzig said—more for himself than for any of them. "Heal up. Then we move."

No one disagreed. But no one looked convinced either.

Conversation dwindled, then faded entirely. The wind picked up high above, whistling through cracks in the cliff—just another reminder of how far they'd fallen.

Slowly, exhaustion claimed them one by one. Ukshagg's scales quivered with each shallow breath, the tension finally slipping from her shoulders. Hashaezkend succumbed to sleep, tears still drying on her face. Shrarzeth fought it stubbornly, eyelids dipping, snapping open, dipping again at every phantom sound. Srezzig leaned back against the rock, closed his eyes, and tried to pretend he was somewhere else—back in the matron's den, before everything had broken.

For a long, brittle hour, no one tried to fill the silence. They simply listened to the night and waited for morning.

The first sound wasn't a roar or a scream or claws raking stone. It was softer than that—something shuffling, deliberate, followed by the careful scrape of hooves on loose gravel. Srezzig's eyes flew open. The cold had slowed him, dulled the edges of instinct, but not enough to stop the surge of adrenaline that snapped him alert. He scanned the darkness, pupils blown wide to drink in every shadow.

All four wyrmlings went silent at once.

The noise crept closer. Then, without warning, something shifted in Hashaezkend's arms. The blink ram Hashaezkend was holding, which had been limp and half-gone, stirred with a low sound. It twitched, then with a shuddering effort, pushed itself onto trembling legs. It stepped into a sliver of moonlight, and as the light touched its coat, its twin horns began to pulse with a faint, internal glow that cast strange patterns across the ravine wall. For a long, breathless moment it stood perfectly still. Didn't twitch. Didn't flinch. It simply watched them.

Ukshagg was on her feet instantly. "That's not possible," she breathed. "It was dying…"

Hashaezkend stared, frozen in place. "It's awake."

Shrarzeth, leaning heavily on her makeshift splint, pressed closer to Srezzig. "What does it want?" Her voice was flat but razor-alert.

The blink ram didn't answer—just took a slow, deliberate step back. Then another. It didn't bolt or blink away. It moved with eerie purpose, eyes locked on the clutch.

Srezzig's first instinct was to lunge, to chase it down before it vanished again—but his body refused. His bad wing shrieked with hot pain before going numb. He managed only to sit up straighter, tail curling protectively around his legs.

The ram paused at the edge of the shelf, then looked back—not toward the moon, not toward escape, but straight at Srezzig. A challenge. Or a plea. Maybe both.

Ukshagg crept forward. "It's leading us," she whispered—half awe, half suspicion.

Srezzig forced himself upright, ignoring the spasm across his ribs. "We don't have another option. We follow, or we die here."

Shrarzeth tucked her broken limb close, shifting awkwardly to three legs. When she wobbled, she steadied herself against Srezzig's good side. "If it's a trap," she murmured, "I'd rather find out on three legs than wait around on four."

The ram moved again. Hashaezkend followed, never letting more than a body-length slip between her and the others, protective instincts flickering across her face.

They trailed it into a narrow side fissure, so tight that even Ukshagg had to duck and crawl. The walls scraped their scales, pinched half-healed wounds, but no one complained. Not even Shrarzeth. Every so often, the ram stopped, turned, stared at them until they caught up—then continued deeper into the mountain.

They traveled maybe half a mile, descending into thicker, mineral-heavy air, the sound of running water growing louder until it drowned out even the wind.

Then the fissure widened into a hidden bowl—an entire hollow chamber carved by time and pressure. Shattered stone columns ringed the walls, and steaming, iridescent pools dotted the ground. Geysers hissed and spat, each one rimmed in mineral crusts of sulfur-yellow, copper-blue, and vivid malachite that cast strange, shifting light across the ceiling. Heat struck them immediately, seeping into frozen joints. Srezzig felt blood move in his limbs again for the first time since dawn.

The blink ram stood at the lip of the largest pool, one hoof perched on a shelf of glittering crystal. It stared at the water, then at them, eyes bright and unnervingly aware.

Ukshagg blinked hard. "This... this isn't on any map."

Shrarzeth eased forward and dipped her paw into a trickle of runoff. The warmth sank deep into her splinted joint, pulling a long breath from her chest.

Hashaezkend crawled to the water's edge, staring at the ripples like she expected them to form a message, a memory, a map of what came next.

The ram watched them without blinking, its body perfectly still. Finally, Ukshagg found her voice. "Why bring us here? You should be terrified of us. But you're not."

Hashaezkend whispered, her eyes unfocused as if listening to something far off. "It wants us to rest. It knows... it knows we're not the only prey out here, just the only ones left who might matter."

Srezzig scanned the chamber, the steam, the fractured stone. "Doesn't change anything. We heal here, or we die out on those rocks."

Ukshagg held the ram's gaze for a long, steady moment, then dipped her head. "Thank you," she said—quiet, unsure if the creature could understand any of it, but needing to speak the gratitude anyway.

The blink ram bowed once in return. Then—liquid as breath, soft as an exhale—it vanished. A faint shimmer hung in the air where it had been, the only proof it was ever there.

The silence that followed felt charged, almost sacred. For the first time in days, warmth settled through the clutch—not just in their bodies, but in the hollow places that fear had carved out. No one spoke. They simply existed, letting the miracle of still being alive wash over them.

Hashaezkend curled beside Shrarzeth, who closed her eyes and eased into the heat. Ukshagg began tracing invisible lines through the geyser field, mapping pathways and pressure zones with her claw, trying to understand the impossible logic that had guided them here. Srezzig sat at the pool's edge, watching his reflection ripple in the blue glow. He looked battered—cracked scales, torn wing, dust in every crease—but he didn't look broken.

Above them, the moon crept across the narrow slice of sky, its pale arc watching over something small and stubborn and worth saving.

In the hidden sanctuary, a stillness settled over the clutch. Srezzig watched his battered reflection ripple in the glowing water, the rising steam blurring his broken edges. Tomorrow they would move again. But for tonight, surrounded by warmth and breathing in the mineral-heavy air, they were simply here. And that was enough.

Chapter 13: The Wyrmling's Gambit

Srezzig woke with a violent jolt—not the slow drift back to consciousness, but his entire body seizing at once, as if sleep had ambushed him. Rest had become a foreign concept. The air reeked of steam and hot metal, thick and oppressive instead of soothing. He dragged himself onto all fours, letting old injuries scream their complaints as he tried to piece together where he was.

Down below, the blink rams drifted through the mist like pale ghosts, their hooves whispering across the mineral-soaked mud. They weren't panicking or bolting—just circling the geyser field in slow, deliberate arcs, as though they knew hunters waited just beyond the steam. Srezzig locked eyes with the largest one, a ram marked by a brilliant blue blaze across its skull. It stared straight back and didn't flinch.

By the water's edge, Ukshagg and Hashaezkend sat close enough that their scales nearly brushed. Ukshagg was checking herself over with mechanical precision—every joint, every claw, every movement cataloged—while Hashaezkend sat utterly still, listening intently to something beneath the constant hiss of boiling vents.

Shrarzeth was the last to wake. She shot upright with a gasp, her bronze scales shimmering with a soft inner light. With a pained grunt, she tore off the splint on her leg and pressed her muzzle to the break. A warm, phosphorescent saliva seeped into the wound. The bone knit itself with a low hum, the flesh sealing over it in seconds. She tested the limb, then moved on to the others, her touch radiating a gentle heat that mended torn scales and dissolved deep bruises.

Each of them flinched as pain flared before dissolving into a spreading warmth. When the final wound vanished, the bright bronze of Shrarzeth's scales had dulled to a soft gray. She let out a long, controlled breath—spent, but deeply satisfied.

They moved through their usual morning routine, but each motion felt hollow, an imitation of normalcy. Aches throbbed under mended scales. Instincts screamed warnings from the steam-shrouded exits. Srezzig tasted adrenaline and scorched stone on his tongue—the flavor of the tomb they had barely escaped. Yesterday's fight was a ghost. Today's survival was the only thing with teeth.

He watched the calm ram again—and something clicked. A lesson from the den, maybe, or something Zaekshilen used to drill into them. Purpose, not fear. Patience over panic.

His reflection wavered in the wet stone, blue-white sparks flickering along his scales. For an instant, the ram's luminous horns seemed to bloom from his own skull.

He hissed under his breath and moved toward the pool's edge. Ukshagg noticed; Hashaezkend's ears twitched. Neither spoke.

Srezzig cleared his throat. "We're not prey. Not yet. You feel it?"

Ukshagg tilted her head, studying him. "You've got a plan." It wasn't quite a question—closer to a warning dressed as hope.

Srezzig flashed a sharp grin. "Always."

A heavy silence settled over them, punctuated only by venting steam. Hashaezkend finally lifted his gaze, exhaustion shadowing the lines of his face. "We're not trapped," he said quietly. "The water connects somewhere."

"That doesn't make sense," Ukshagg muttered.

"It's what I'm feeling," Hashaezkend insisted, voice thin but certain.

Srezzig let the stillness stretch before tapping the slick mud with one claw. "The blink rams—they move like prey, but they're not acting like it. They stay here because they know what's hunting them can't follow. Not in a place like this."

Ukshagg snorted. "So what, we pretend to be rams?"

"No," Srezzig said. "We use them."

Ukshagg barked out a laugh—part amusement, part disbelief. "And how do you suggest we do that?"

Srezzig scratched a rough map into the mud, showing their cavern and the narrow exit passage above. "The horde is waiting up there. Rams blink when they're cornered. What if we drive them up that passage, right at the Undragons?"

Hashaezkend's eyes widened. "A living wall of teleporting flesh."

"Pure chaos," Srezzig corrected. "We make the Undragons think the rams are trying to break out. While they're dealing with dozens of blinking targets, we slip out through the geothermal vents Hashaezkend feels. The steam and chaos will buy us time."

Ukshagg studied the sketch. "Half of us can barely stand."

Srezzig turned to Shrarzeth. "Can you handle it?"

Shrarzeth swallowed, sparks flickering across her claws. "I can try."

Ukshagg tapped the spiral he'd drawn. "What about timing?"

Srezzig met her gaze. "We set it off the moment the matron shows herself. One mistake and—"

"We're dead," Hashaezkend finished, voice flat.

"This is what I saw," Hashaezkend whispered suddenly. "Steam and light. Rams first. Then us. Then the monsters."

Ukshagg traced the lines again, slower this time. "The Undragons will go after the biggest threat. If the rams blink all at once, it'll overload their senses. We'd get maybe three—four seconds."

Srezzig nodded. "Not much. But enough."

"Better than nothing," Shrarzeth said, voice steadier than before.

Silence settled again as each of them weighed the odds. Then Ukshagg gave a sharp nod. "We'll need to time it with the geysers. Use the steam to mask our scent."

Shrarzeth walked to the largest blink ram. It watched her approach without fear. "I think it trusts me," she murmured. "Or maybe it just knows I'm terrified."

Srezzig carved one last spiral into the mud, then looked at his clutchmates—all battered, all trembling, but all still standing. "Rest now," he said. "Then we rehearse until we could do it in our sleep."

Maybe it was madness. But in the blue-white glow of the steam, their desperation almost looked like brilliance.

The rams kept circling, their movements a slow, patient dance. The wyrmlings huddled close, their shadows stretched long and strange by the light. For the first time in days, Srezzig felt something like hope crawl up through his scales and settle in his chest.

He'd be ready.

And when the monsters came, he would not be prey.

Chapter 14: Clash of Scales and Shadows

The killing field waited—silent, steaming, sharpened to a point—while Srezzig scanned the sky for omens that stubbornly refused to show. This wasn't a hunt. Not even a skirmish. This was a line carved in blood with extinction crouched on the far side, and Srezzig stood at its razor edge.

Below him, the world boiled. The geyser bowl yawned wide, mud crusted over from the last eruption, its edges bristling with obsidian teeth. Blink rams circled the caldera in desperate, tightening bands, their blue-white coats matted and streaked with filth. They moved with the frantic logic of cornered prey, their hooves carving jagged, desperate lines into the mud—a language of pure survival.

Ukshagg perched on a vent to his right, claws sunk deep into the stone, head low. She never stopped scanning the steam—cataloging every flicker, every silhouette that wavered at the edge of sight. Sometimes a pale twin shimmered beside her, either testing her fading magic or warning away whatever watched from the mist. Srezzig and Ukshagg didn't exchange a word. They didn't need to. They'd run this plan until it had fused into muscle and bone.

Near the southern rim, Hashaezkend made herself small behind a ring of weather-blasted volcanic rock. Her pearl-white scales blended into the chalky stone, but Srezzig could *feel* her tension—every breath, every twitch—like a second heartbeat running under the ground. She hovered over the pressure points of the largest blink ram, talons poised just inches from its trembling flank. The beast stood frozen at the cliff's lip, bracing for whatever impossible thing came next.

On the opposite boundary, Shrarzeth paced in tight, vicious ovals—every step a promise, every exhale a challenge. Acid lingered on her tongue, though her jaws stayed clamped. Bronze scales caught the fractured light in the bowl's cracks, leaving faint afterimages that trailed behind her like ghosts. Srezzig watched her, waiting for the moment she would matter most.

Then the wind shifted—cold enough to slice the mist clean off the stone.

Srezzig tensed and lashed his tail once: *ready.*

Around the caldera, every clutchmate snapped to attention.

Ukshagg and Hashaezkend shared a single glance—tiny, fast, but enough—and moved.

Ukshagg's volley hit first: a ripple of gold light. Threads spun from her claws, anchoring themselves into steam and stone until three, then six, then a dozen phantom wyrmlings burst across the field. Each illusion ran perfect loops, baiting the rams' terrified eyes—mimicking Ukshagg's grace with almost insulting accuracy. The Undragons faltered, jaws trembling, torn between hunger and the flicker of false prey. Confusion rolled through the ranks like a brushfire.

Hashaezkend struck next. She drew a wavering breath, then released it in a pulse of raw force that shook the ground. Mud erupted, and a fissure spiderwebbed from the impact point. Three rams stumbled. The Undragons flinched, scales rippling as brutes with shattered jaws shrieked at nothing. The line buckled before the charge even began.

The ground trembled—something massive, something fast, closing in.

Srezzig's claws dug into the stone. Time to move.

"Ukshagg, Shrarzeth—left flank! Hashaezkend, with me!" he roared.

Shrarzeth didn't hesitate. She pivoted hard, spat a stream of blistering acid that hissed across the mud, then launched herself at the nearest Undragon with a scream full of teeth and fury. The lead monster braced, but its companions—tripped up by Ukshagg's illusions—never saw her coming. Shrarzeth hit low, rolled under a swipe, then carved a deadly arc of acid that splattered across three throats at once.

The air filled with the wet, vicious hiss of burning scale.

Ukshagg's phantoms doubled, then quadrupled—until hundreds of gold-glowing wyrmlings flooded the field. They wove through the blink rams in shimmering arcs, every spectral body baiting the monsters into useless chases. The real Ukshagg drifted among them, always one shimmer ahead of snapping jaws, moving like a golden heartbeat pulsing through the chaos.

Hashaezkend fired a second pulse, pitched just above pain. It ricocheted off the stone, sending rams blinking in raw panic and short-circuiting three smaller Undragons at once. One flailed mid-blink and slammed into dead wood. Another rolled onto its back and curled up, sobbing through broken teeth. The bowl erupted into pure, unfiltered mayhem.

Then the matron came.

She tore through the southern rim, the steam parting for a face that looked large enough to split the sky. Twice the height of legend, she wore scales like dented armor, thick plates split with oozing seams of black oil. Half her skull lay bare—bone and nerve exposed—and her jaw hung open in a permanent, silent scream. A chorus of every wyrm she had ever devoured unfurled across the killing field in one soul-shaking wave.

Even Shrarzeth flattened to the ground.

Ukshagg's phantoms flickered—but she forced them back into cohesion, sending a dozen golden copies streaking toward the matron's eyes. The beast inhaled, then exhaled a single blast of ice-cold air that froze blink rams mid-step and shattered two phantoms on impact.

Hashaezkend absorbed the aftershock, turned it, then hurled it forward. The pulse ricocheted off the matron's exposed bone with a crack that echoed through the basin. The monster jerked back, and the panicked rams blinked as one—a tidal wave of blue-white light that blinded everything still clinging to life.

Srezzig watched the cracks spiderweb through the horde, then locked onto the matron's ruined skull. She hesitated—just for a heartbeat—and something like indecision flickered behind her burned-out eye.

He saw his opening.

Shrarzeth and Ukshagg converged on the left rim, cutting off the matron's escape. Shrarzeth's acid struck armored joints, sizzling through flesh that smoked and steamed. Ukshagg spun her phantoms into a tightening spiral, each spectral wyrmling baiting another savage, desperate snap.

Srezzig and Hashaezkend scrambled up the upper ledge, claws tearing into frozen stone. The matron swung a massive forelimb, crushing two phantoms and catching one very real Shrarzeth. The bronze wyrmling tumbled hard but didn't break. Ukshagg seized the opening, unleashing a blistering barrage of gold light at the matron's exposed flank. The hits rippled through her like something inside was trying to claw its way out.

When the beast lifted her head, Srezzig leapt.

His half-torn wing barely held as he cut through scalding steam, soaring over gaping jaws.

"Now!" he roared.

Hashaezkend's pulse struck the bare skull—timed perfectly with Srezzig's diving form—and detonated in a shattering wave. The matron howled as her body locked in violent spasms. Below, the blink rams flickered in one blinding blaze that swallowed the entire bowl whole.

Srezzig hit the ground ten paces away, crackling with raw, unstable energy. The matron lifted her ruined gaze to his—and for the first time, fear glinted in her shattered eyes.

Srezzig smiled. Slow. Deliberate.

He had drawn first blood.

For a heartbeat, the matron froze. Then her jaw unhinged, releasing a shriek so violent it tore through the clouds and stripped the mist from the air as she lunged forward with terrible, single-minded purpose.

Srezzig felt the shockwave in his bones first—then the teeth. The matron's first step sent boiling mud spraying thirty feet in every direction; the second made the entire rim convulse, shaking so hard even Ukshagg's illusions flickered and buckled.

But Srezzig was already moving.

He darted in from the side, jaws clamping hard onto the monster's exposed forelimb joint. A pulse of raw static burst from his fangs, crackling across the armored scales, bleaching them white before splintering down toward the marrow. The matron shrieked and whipped her skull around, jaws gaping—but Srezzig had already tumbled free, tail flicking an insolent challenge from just beyond her reach.

"Coward!" the matron snarled, but the word came out half-formed— more instinct than thought.

Ukshagg seized the opening. With a burst of magic that nearly dropped her to one knee, she launched four new phantoms straight at the matron's exposed face. Two Undragons, fooled by the shimmering mirage, collided at full speed, crashing down in a tangle of claws and broken teeth. A third, sharper than the others, blinked through the illusion—its gaze locking onto Ukshagg directly.

Each time they returned, they came back differently.

Srezzig tucked that detail aside and lunged.

Ukshagg barely rolled clear as three Undragons struck her perch at once. The air sizzled with corrupted flame; her gold scales went white-hot, then charred black as she dropped low, letting the steam swallow her outline. The trio overshot, jaws snapping at empty air—just in time for Ukshagg to rise behind them and slam the nearest one with a headbutt to the spine. The wyrmling tumbled end over end until it plunged into the scalding geyser pool below. The water erupted in a towering plume of steam, carrying a wail that twisted, thinned, and died.

Hashaezkend moved like a ghost—silent, but everywhere at once. Each time an Undragon squad tried to rally, she was there above them, unleashing a shriek so razor-precise it split the difference between pain and panic. The monsters staggered, ears bleeding, scales trembling as formation after formation broke apart. Hashaezkend's voice cracked once, her whole body faltering, but the next shriek came sharper, louder, and the Undragons recoiled in fear.

The blink rams were going wild now. Every roar from the matron or burst of magic sent them teleporting in frantic, unpredictable waves— sometimes five or six at a time, other times an entire herd in a synchronized blue-white pop. Undragons lunged for them, only to find open air, then crashed into their own squadmates or skidded headfirst into boiling pools. Even Srezzig, trying to track what was real versus illusion, almost lost his bearings once and had to slow mid-dive before the steam swallowed him whole.

Shrarzeth was everywhere and nowhere at once—a streak of bronze slicing through the white steam. Each time a wyrmling took a hit, she materialized beside them, claws blazing with healing energy as she patched wounds on the fly. When the matron's tail lashed out, it caught Srezzig across the flank, tearing a hole so wide his scales flared red. Shrarzeth dropped from the sky, wrapped him in a pulse of raw life, and the wound sealed shut in an instant—leaving her own bronze scales a shade duller as the matron's tail slammed uselessly into empty air.

Ukshagg spared half a heartbeat to marvel. "You're insane," she muttered, but Shrarzeth was already gone, streaking toward her next patient.

The matron grew angrier, and the battlefield warped around her fury. The Undragons shifted tactics, moving in tight pairs now, forcing the clutch backward step by step. The lesser monsters—smaller, faster, and far more desperate—threw themselves into the fray, sacrificing flesh and bone to draw fire or confuse phantoms so the matron could keep advancing. Srezzig saw the pattern, recognized the trap, and decided to break the entire game.

"Stay with me. Ukshagg—pin the center. Hashaezkend—hit the leader. Shrarzeth—keep us alive."

With a snarl, Srezzig ramped his static discharge to maximum. He leapt from vent to vent, always keeping the matron's injured leg in sight, and struck it three times in rapid succession. Each jolt cooked another layer of scale away, exposing rotten, pulsing flesh beneath.

Ukshagg, still reeling from the earlier barrage, focused every scrap of will she had left and cast one perfect illusion—a second matron, full size, roaring from the opposite side of the bowl. The real beast hesitated—just long enough for Ukshagg and Srezzig to strike from both sides at once.

Hashaezkend's next shriek was her strongest yet. Its frequency hit the exposed tissue along the matron's skull, making the monster's entire body lock rigid. Across the battlefield, lesser Undragons seized for a heartbeat—coordination shattering—and three of them pitched into boiling pools or snapped their own necks in the chaos.

Then the blink rams went wild.

An entire herd popped into existence on the matron's back, their tiny hooves scrabbling for purchase. The nearest ram lowered its head and pressed its horn to the exposed flesh. A burst of light detonated where it touched, the wound sizzling with displacement energy. The matron howled as warped magic shredded her cells from the inside out.

More rams flickered onto her skin, each horn-touch leaving behind a crater of twisted, collapsing tissue. The matron snapped at them, but each time her jaws closed, the rams blinked away—reappearing elsewhere with their horns already driving into new vulnerable spots. The battlefield dissolved into a nightmare of light flashes, teleport cracks, and agonized roars.

Srezzig saw the new pattern instantly. The matron was losing control of her body, but the mind—the hateful, calculating mind—was still there. The next move would have to be flawless.

He leapt.

Timing his jump with a geyser's updraft and the synchronized blink of an entire herd, Srezzig rode the steam upward, gaining precious altitude. The distracted matron never looked up. The blue wyrmling dropped out of the haze, hit her spine hard, dug in with all four claws, and sank his teeth straight into the exposed nerve along her neck.

The taste was electric—rot, blood, power, and hate all tangled into one furious jolt. Srezzig's jaws locked down, and with a pulse of raw static, he fired a bolt strong enough to light the entire caldera for a heartbeat.

The matron arched violently, her whole body contorting as the energy ripped through her. She flung Srezzig off like he weighed nothing. He hit the ground, rolled through the mud, and slid to a stop—bruised, battered, but not broken.

The beast staggered, then whipped back around, baring every jagged tooth in her ruined maw. She was dying, but her haunches were already coiling for another lunge.

Srezzig glanced upward. Storm clouds churned overhead, thick with static. He felt the charge ripple along his spine, every hair on his body standing straight. The battlefield—mud, geysers, steam, rams, illusions—had become a living circuit.

All it needed was a trigger.

"Ukshagg!" Srezzig roared. "Now!"

Running on fumes and desperation, Ukshagg summoned her last perfect shimmer—a spiral of blinking rams, a whole herd of gold-lit illusions flickering around the matron's massive head. The Undragons spun with them, confused beyond reason, chasing the phantoms in a frenzied loop.

In that chaos, Hashaezkend unleashed one final, impossible shriek—so sharp it cracked a fissure through the bowl and rattled the stone under their feet. Even the rams flinched, teleporting at random like sparks jumping a wire.

Shrarzeth darted in, patched the final wound along Srezzig's ribs with a pulse of healing fire, then rolled him behind the nearest vent before the next shockwave hit.

Srezzig braced himself, gathered every scrap of energy left in his body, and spat a concentrated bolt of static directly into the matron's exposed left eye.

It hit.

The monster shrieked—an earth-splitting, marrow-deep howl—and lurched sideways. The blast shattered scale and sinew, blowing the socket open and exposing bone beneath. Her left foreleg buckled completely, collapsing under her own weight as she dropped hard onto her front limbs. Steam erupted beneath her as she fought to stand.

Srezzig saw the opening. Felt the charge building. The world narrowed to a singular, electric point.

The matron stared at him—rage flickering in what remained of her eyes, something like recognition trembling behind it.

"Prey," she rasped, her voice a dying wind scraping across stone.

Srezzig smiled, teeth crackling with light, a grin full of storm and war.

"Not today," he said.

The sky split open in a blaze of electric fire, and the matron braced herself to face the storm.

The matron's failing body shuddered, but the mind behind her eyes still had teeth. She roared, and what poured from her jaws wasn't sound—it was a spray of corrupted flame, black and oily, hot enough to melt stone. Srezzig rolled clear as the blast set the air ablaze.

As the matron inhaled for another attack, Ukshagg pushed out one final illusion: a ring of Srezzigs charging from every direction. The monster spun, jaws snapping at shadows. High above, Hashaezkend let out a sonic shriek so sharp it sliced through stone. The blink rams heard it and blinked in a flawless, synchronized spiral, their teleportation magic crackling in the air.

Srezzig felt the charge building, a perfect line through the chaos. Lightning crawled across the storm's belly, mirroring the static rising on his own scales. This was it. He opened his jaws, and with a roar that matched the storm, let the power loose.

It surged through the battlefield—not from the sky, but through his clutch. Ukshagg's illusions, Hashaezkend's shriek, the rams' teleportation— each current threaded into Srezzig's body. His chest glowed with borrowed energy before he hurled a javelin of lightning straight into the matron's shattered skull.

The sound wasn't a bang—it was a tearing, as if the world itself was being ripped apart. The matron froze, then convulsed, her body seizing so violently the stone beneath her cracked. For a long, awful second she teetered, suspended between life and ruin. Then she collapsed.

burned hollow. He rolled to a stop near the caldera's edge, claws digging into ash. For a second, he let himself think it was truly over.

Then the sky broke open.

The storm—held back for so long—finally dropped its charge. Lightning hammered the ground, striking the matron's corpse again and again. Each bolt sent a ripple of energy across the field, causing the remaining Undragons to shudder and collapse, their connection to their leader severed.

The world went silent. Only the hiss of cooling stone remained.

Ukshagg, eyes half-rolled back, limped over and collapsed beside Srezzig. "That was... not in the plan," she muttered, voice stuck between a laugh and a sob.

Hashaezkend drifted down, wings trembling, and folded herself close. Shrarzeth limped in last, every patch of her scales still glowing with spent heat. No one spoke. There was nothing left to say.

The blink rams, no longer terrified, edged back into the clearing. They moved cautiously, but when they saw the clutch, they didn't bolt. The largest—the one with the blue blaze—approached Srezzig, touched its horns to his chest, and for a moment the two simply breathed together.

Srezzig looked at his clutchmates—battered, burnt, but alive. "We hold here," he said softly, but his voice didn't waver. "No more running."

The others nodded. Even Ukshagg looked strangely at peace.

Above, the clouds parted, letting a shaft of sunlight fall across the battlefield—so pure it hurt to look at. The killing field, once nothing but death, now steamed with the first fragile promise of something else.

For the first time, Srezzig let himself believe in what came after.

The world outside went on, indifferent, waiting for nothing.

Chapter 15: Wings of Change

The caldera floor was still smoking. Even dead, the monsters kept bleeding—steam and rot hissing out of burst flesh, that iron-electric stench that had clung to Windscour Cliffs since the matron fell. Srezzig stood at the center. He wasn't tall—nothing here was—but every scale on his back crackled with the echo of what he'd just done.

His blue wing hung wrong, the membrane torn and crusted with dried blood. He flexed a claw. Sparks danced along his knuckles. Some kind of reward, he figured. Didn't feel like one.

His clutchmates came to him one by one. Ukshagg circled the perimeter first, gold scales filthy but intact, each step trailing half a dozen phantom copies. You never knew which one was real. She made sure of that. Hashaezkend followed, throat humming with the remnants of a song. Her scales were battered, but her eyes stayed fixed on Srezzig. Shrarzeth came last, moving on all fours, healing light flickering at her claws like the last warmth in the caldera.

For a breath, there was only wind.

Srezzig shook the charge from his limbs. "Ukshagg—eastern tunnels. Hashaezkend, prep sonic. Shrarzeth—no heroics. Clean and fast."

Ukshagg's afterimages shivered with amusement. "You'd know if I ever hesitated," she whispered.

Hashaezkend flinched at the pooled blood but lifted her head, nostrils flaring. Shrarzeth pressed a glowing claw to the torn edge of Srezzig's wing. A quiet chant sealed the ragged membrane, leaving it tender but whole.

They moved together.

Ukshagg vanished into illusion ahead—gold ghosts splitting and re-forming in the heat shimmer. Hashaezkend's hum rippled behind them, soft but sharp enough to make the steam quiver. Shrarzeth drifted along the flanks, mending what she could and watching the shadows with healer's suspicion.

At the caldera's edge, Srezzig halted. The tunnel mouth gaped, black and wet. He met each of their eyes—Ukshagg's steady focus, Hashaezkend's resolute nod, Shrarzeth's unwavering gaze. The grudges that once divided them felt like ash; all that mattered was that they were still here. "We finish this," he said. "No lingering."

Shrarzeth flexed her claws, the healing light at their tips hardening into something fierce. "Lead."

They dropped into the tunnel. Stale air. The smell of monster fat. The horror of what they'd almost become. None of it slowed them.

Ukshagg's illusions scouted every branch, spooking Undragon guards into abandoning their posts. Hashaezkend shattered stalactites with precise sonic pulses to collapse ambush points. Shrarzeth kept tight to their sides, sealing cuts before they bled.

Past the first bend the tunnel widened into switchbacks. Rumbles shook pebbles loose—aftershocks from the matron's death. Srezzig listened for movement deeper in.

"Ukshagg—clutch room."

Her phantoms answered through overlapping mouths: "Left fork, past two cave-ins, then down. You'll smell it—like lightning struck rot."

The illusions darted ahead, luring guards into empty corridors. Hashaezkend's whispers nudged loose boulders into choke points. When a mid-sized Undragon lunged from a side tunnel, she met it with a sonic blast that shattered bone like crystal. The beast shrieked and staggered.

Srezzig finished it with a headbutt that rattled its skull and silenced it for good.

"Left fork. Slow. Prep pulse. Shrarzeth—backstop."

The clutch moved as one, a four-headed hunter flowing through the dark, their purpose a single sharp point.

They reached the shattered archive vault in three minutes. Scraps of bone and rotted logic lay buried under the debris. Nothing stirred. Shrarzeth sent out a ripple of healing light to check for survivors, but only silence—thick, old, absolute—answered.

Then the ground shuddered. Pebbles rattled loose.

"Down!" Srezzig roared.

The clutch flattened, wings folding tight. A hulking Undragon burst through the broken arch—twice the size of the others, corrupted scales oozing black ichor in thick ropes. It reared back, acid dripping from exposed fangs like venom ready to choose a target.

Ukshagg's phantoms baited it, flickering in and out like golden ghosts, but this one was smarter than the rest. It swept its barbed tail straight through the illusions, scattering them like dust, then charged directly at Shrarzeth. Hashaezkend snapped up a sonic shield that shattered falling boulders into harmless grit. Shrarzeth pressed against the wall, healing light dimming to a frightened quiver.

The Undragon lunged. Srezzig leapt—but his injured wing threw him off balance. He slammed into a pillar as the monster's jaws snapped shut inches from Shrarzeth's throat.

A black blur tore through the chamber.

Drozkax—appearing from a side tunnel like a nightmare reborn—slammed into the Undragon's flank. His obsidian scales were crisscrossed with fresh pink scars where they'd been peeled back during captivity. He gleamed with sweat as he drove the beast backward. One eye was swollen shut, but the other burned with raw fury as his claws—three missing on his left foreleg—ripped furrows into the corrupted hide.

"Not my clutch!" he roared, voice thick, ragged, and furious.

Three stragglers lunged into the chamber behind the alpha. The team struck without needing orders: Ukshagg severed a hamstring with surgical precision, Hashaezkend's screech sent a concussive wave that shattered eardrums and their balance, and Srezzig snapped the last skull with one brutal strike.

Drozkax and the alpha tumbled together in a death spiral, smashing through stone shelves and broken archives. The black wyrmling's jaws found the soft spot beneath the monster's jaw. One savage twist. A wet, final crack.

The Undragon went limp.

Drozkax stood unsteadily, chest heaving, black scales slick with ichor. Raw pink flesh glistened where scales had been methodically removed, forming a grotesque pattern across his flank. His left eye remained swollen shut, crusted with dried blood.

"Miss me?" he growled through a jaw that didn't quite close right anymore.

Silence followed. Dust drifted like falling shrouds. Not a breath stirred.

Drozkax sagged against the wall, his breath a raw, labored sound. "They... collect things." His good eye narrowed, fixing on a glint of broken crystal on the floor. "My scales."

He shuddered. "They talked," he rasped. "Not like... animals. A system."

"Tremors started. They ran. I broke free." His claws flexed, the missing three leaving phantom impressions in the dust. "Tracked the lightning. And the healing."

Srezzig turned to his clutch—bloodied, exhausted, unbroken. He flexed his wounded wing, winced, and straightened.

"We go home."

They rose, battered but united. Ukshagg's illusions faded into the dim. Hashaezkend lowered her head, trembling with spent power. Shrarzeth closed her eyes, her glow flickering like the last ember of a long night.

They pushed back through the tunnels as the world trembled behind them. Collapse sealed passageways, but together they found every twisted turn. At last they burst into daylight just as the rock went silent.

No one cheered. There was only the weight of what it had cost them, and the particular silence of people who had paid it. The sun climbed higher, indifferent to their scars. They stood at the edge of the world, something meaner now, sharper, carrying their dead in the set of their jaws.

Srezzig spread his wings once, stiff with grief.

"We carry them," he said, voice low and steady as stone. "Always."

They turned away from the cliffs—clutch together, bound by what they'd faced, and by what they had become.

The blink rams had bunched up at the edge—maybe two dozen of them—coats still caked with mud and old blood from the killing field. They stood there shivering despite the afternoon sun, frost clinging stubbornly to their horns, flinching at every drifting shadow. Srezzig could see the panic written in every tight muscle, and he felt it mirrored in the hollow space inside his own chest—right where Zaekshilen's steadiness used to sit.

He flicked his tail—barely enough movement to matter—then cleared his throat. When he spoke, his voice came out low and roughened by exhaustion and grief.

"Drozkax, perimeter. Ukshagg, herd them with light—no ghosts. Hashaezkend, soothe them. Shrarzeth, medic."

Even as the words left his mouth, he wondered if he would ever feel certain again. But the team moved anyway.

Drozkax circled to the far side of the herd, planting himself between the rams and the cliff drop. The black wyrmling flinched once at his own shadow—then overcorrected with a snarl so sharp it sent the nearest rams scattering like startled birds. His scales shuddered under the strain before he caught himself, inhaled sharply, and reset his stance. When he looked up again, his lone good eye swept constantly—herd, horizon, back again—as if he were trying to find the line between protecting them and becoming the very thing they feared.

Ukshagg traced the opposite side, fingertips glowing with faint, muted illusion. This time he kept it simple—just soft color shifts, hints of green grass and safe ground ahead. No towering phantoms, no tricks sharp enough to spook. The rams leaned toward the changing light, drawn by the promise of something gentler.

Hashaezkend knelt in front of the first trembling ram, her breathing controlled and quiet, voice folding into a gentle hum. She pushed empathy into the space between them until the ram blinked, hesitated, and finally folded its legs beneath itself with something like relief. For a moment her eyes went glassy with tears—for the creature trembling before her, and for the heavy silence that had settled over their clutch.

Shrarzeth moved through the herd with focused calm, checking for injuries. She found one ram with a shattered foreleg—bone jutting through the skin at a vicious angle. Her claws lit blue-white as she wrapped healing magic around the break, coaxing flesh and bone back together until the limb sealed with a soft, satisfying pop. The ram stood, weight-tested its leg, then rejoined the others with a stubborn determination that felt almost holy.

Srezzig stayed at the edge, shoulders tight, the weight of his command as heavy as any stone. He swallowed hard and forced his voice steadier than he felt.

"Not done yet. Move them out."

They moved. Ukshagg and Drozkax took point, Srezzig and Hashaezkend wove through the center, and Shrarzeth brought up the rear with the newly healed ram. At first the herd shuffled forward with their heads down, still spooked by every stray sound. But as they continued up the path, something shifted—tails lifting, steps growing more certain.

By the time they turned onto the ridge trail, the rams moved like one continuous line: trusting the path, the rhythm, and the gap in the line that none of them moved to fill.

Chapter 16: Return to Fallen Scale Peaks

Dawn split the sky open. Srezzig flew point, his shadow stretching long and sharp through the clouds below while his clutchmates fanned out behind him. Their wings cut through the air in silent, practiced sync, each stroke pulling at muscles that remembered every mile and every wound. Blue lightning flickered between Srezzig's scales now and then, tracing his ribs—the power still humming inside him, proof of what he'd become and what it had cost.

Down below, the blink rams moved as one mass, a pale blue-white stream flowing across the jagged ridges. They teleported in quick jumps—pop of ozone, blur of afterimage, tiny static shocks rippling through the thin mountain air. Even the stragglers had stopped trying to veer off on their own; survival had taught them better. The rams followed the dragons. The dragons followed Srezzig.

Flying hurt. Srezzig's wing throbbed with every beat, static crackling beneath the awkwardly healed membrane. He ignored it, feeling the rhythm of the others behind him—Ukshagg's ragged breath, Hashaezkend's wavering effort. They were all wounded, all exhausted, but they flew as one. This flight would prove what survival had made of them.

The Fallen Scale Peaks jutted up ahead like broken teeth. Srezzig knew those edges by heart. He could picture the home ridge's old shelf perfectly: the cracked stone webbing outward like dried lightning, the circle of petrified claws jutting up from the ledge, the scattered scales they'd shed as juveniles. The mountains hadn't changed. But Srezzig and his clutch? They were new creatures wearing old skins.

Hashaezkend pulled up beside him, eyes bloodshot, scales dull and flat. "You good?" she rasped.

"Doesn't matter," he said. "Keep them tight."

"They're not going anywhere." She dipped her head toward the rams below. "You think they know what's coming?"

Srezzig considered it. "They're prey. They always know."

She nodded once, weary and sharp, then drifted back to keep the others in line. For a moment Srezzig flew alone. He let his wings find the old rhythm without thinking, the one his body still knew even if every downstroke cost him now, and tried to remember when that rhythm had been effortless. Then he pulled himself back, because that world was gone and wasn't coming back.

Something cut through the clouds ahead—fast. Too fast.

"Contact," Ukshagg hissed. Ukshagg never sounded surprised, but she did now.

The shape barreled straight toward them. Srezzig locked his wings and barked, "On me." The clutch tightened instantly, the rams clustering below in a jittery mass. The shadow grew with every heartbeat until it burst through the clouds and split the sky with a single colossal wingbeat.

Shyvnir. Her wings blotted out the sun as she filled the sky, so much bigger than he remembered. She was a wall of hammered bronze, her face carved deeper with scars from battles he'd never known. This was their mother, the matron who'd taught him he could be more than something else's meal.

She dove once, impossibly fast, then circled the formation, her roar shaking every bone, every plume of air, every instinct they'd ever learned. Her voice held every order, every warning, every unspoken threat that had shaped Srezzig into something hard enough to endure. Even Drozkax flinched, scales pulling tight as the sound rolled over them.

Shyvnir banked hard, then stopped dead in the updraft. She hung there in the open air, massive wings catching the wind with effortless control, her head tilting as she stared at them with something like disbelief.

The clutch hovered beneath her, barely breathing.

Finally, she spoke—and her words hit like stones. "You're alive."

Srezzig managed a smile, thin and crooked. "Not for lack of trying."

Shyvnir's gaze swept over them, lightning-sharp. She took in the wound in Srezzig's wing—the ragged seam still glowing with dried blood and crackling static. She saw the battered smear along Ukshagg's side, the gold dulled almost to gray. Hashaezkend's ribs—broken, healed crooked. Drozkax's acid-etched scars running down his neck. Shrarzeth's leg wrapped in fresh membrane, bronze scales wet with new growth.

She saw all of it. And her eyes widened—not with pride. Not yet.

"What did you do?" she asked, her voice dropping low, the tone electric and dangerous.

Ukshagg—brave now in a way she hadn't been before—called out, "We lived. We fought. We won."

Shyvnir snorted, a sound like thunder cracking along stone. "Fought what?"

Drozkax answered, without fully meeting her gaze. "Monsters. Bigger than you'd believe. Maybe even bigger than you."

A pause. Srezzig thought he caught a flicker—almost amusement.

"I doubt that," she said, but her voice had softened, the old edges blunted.

They hung there together: a circle of battered survivors and a matron who had counted them as ghosts. Srezzig watched her face as the truth settled in, the hard lines of her jaw softening fractionally. This wasn't the clutch she had raised. This was something new. Something the world had tried to kill and failed.

Slowly, she folded her wings, a gesture of truce. She dipped her head—a minuscule bow of respect—before spreading them wide again. Then she roared, and the sound was not a challenge but a summons: a deep, resonant call home.

Srezzig led the clutch into her wake, the five of them tucking in tight. Shyvnir dipped her tail as she passed, brushing each of them in turn. A steady, grounding touch for Srezzig. Quick and approving for Ukshagg. Gentle, then firm, for Hashaezkend. A playful swat for Drozkax that nearly knocked him sideways. And for Shrarzeth—a long, careful sweep that seemed to say: you made it.

They soared over the ridge, light painting everything in gold and blue. The blink rams settled below, their bodies folding into the stone like they had finally found someplace safe. Srezzig glanced at the matron, then at his clutch, feeling the weight of everything they had survived—every wound, every loss, every impossible moment they had clawed their way through.

But mostly, he felt small again.

Not weak or scared. It wasn't awe, either, but scale. Next to the sheer presence of Shyvnir, the sky felt like a cage. He didn't just want to conquer the peaks; he wanted every horizon she commanded, and all the ones beyond.

The clutch banked together, bodies cutting through the wind as one. Behind them, the rams stamped and waited. Ahead, the nest rose, glowing with the promise of rest, reunion, and whatever came next.

Srezzig let electricity gather along his wing, let it burn warm beneath the healing membrane. For a moment he allowed himself to believe in the future—bright, unbroken, theirs.

Then he tucked his chin, fixed his gaze on the horizon, and flew home.

They touched down as one, claws scraping a controlled skid across the cracked stone of the home nest. The blink rams stumbled in after them—skittish but cooperating—like they'd finally understood who was in charge. The clutch formed a ragged semicircle, everyone watching Mother Shyvnir as she settled onto the highest rock, wings tucked tight, tail hanging down the ledge like a verdict waiting to be spoken.

Nobody said anything at first. Coming home—none of them had really thought about what that would feel like. Even the wind seemed to pause, and the rams pressed themselves deep into the shadows at the far end of the nest.

Ukshagg went first. She was limping, clearly favoring her left side, but her eyes stayed fixed on the matron. She lifted one claw—the movement deliberate and painful—and said, "You wanted proof. Here it is."

The gold wyrmling flicked her wrist. The air above the nest shimmered, and a single phantom took shape: the massive Undragon matron, skull half-exposed. A second illusion formed—Srezzig, wreathed in lightning, delivering the final blow. The tableau hung there for three heartbeats, then dissolved into scattered dust motes.

Ukshagg bowed. Not deeply, but enough.

Mother Shyvnir watched her limp back to her place, the first pale light of dawn catching along Ukshagg's battered scales.

Hashaezkend went next. She knelt beside the nearest blink ram, which shook so hard its horns clattered against the stone. She didn't speak. She just laid her paw on its head and pressed gently until the trembling stilled. The ram blinked once, twice—then relaxed, breathing easy, as though fear had slipped off its shoulders. Hashaezkend rose slowly, exhaustion dragging at her limbs, but she managed a small, genuine smile at the matron.

Shyvnir nodded, something subtle and soft warming her expression.

Shrarzeth could barely keep her posture, but she carried herself like she had every right to stand center. She walked to the heart of the nest, every step a private battle, then gestured toward the herd behind her. "We brought them back," she said. "Figured out how they move. How they disappear." She glanced at Srezzig, then Ukshagg, Drozkax, Hashaezkend—as though she were seeing them as family for the very first time. "We can use this. Nothing gets through a defense like that."

Mother Shyvnir's mouth twitched. "Show me."

The bronze wyrmling grinned and barked a short command at the rams. The three closest blinked at once—reappearing at the nest's edge, then at the base of the outcropping, then right at the matron's feet. They blinked calmly, utterly unafraid, and nuzzled her claws before vanishing again and popping back into place beside the herd.

The matron let out a long, measured breath. The clutch felt her pride even though she still hadn't spoken it aloud.

Then Drozkax stepped forward.

His head was low, tail dragging; the black scales along his spine were cracked and crusted with dried blood. For a moment, Srezzig thought he might bolt—or lash out. Instead, Drozkax said, simply, "I was wrong."

Silence wrapped the nest.

"I thought being cruel was survival," he continued, still avoiding their eyes. "Figured if I hurt people first, nothing could touch me." He looked up then, just once, at the matron, his gaze raw. "But I saw those monsters. Saw what happens when you don't stop yourself. You become something you can't come back from." His tail flicked, acid sizzling where it struck the dirt. "I don't want that. Not for us. Not for me."

He finally looked up and held Shyvnir's gaze. "I'm sorry," he said. "For before. For everything."

The matron's eyes narrowed. For a heartbeat, Srezzig was certain she'd tear into him—say the one thing that would shatter whatever was left of Drozkax. Instead, she closed her eyes—a slow, deliberate blink—and turned her head a fraction away from him. It wasn't exactly approval, but it was the closest the old wyrm had ever come to forgiveness.

Srezzig had watched all of it in silence. He didn't need to speak—he'd always been the shield, the one who absorbed the first blow, the one who decided when it was safe to breathe again. So he just stood there, the charge in his wing crackling every few seconds, electricity sparking whenever the memories cut too close.

Mother Shyvnir turned her steel-blue eyes on him. "You kept them together," she said. Not a question.

"I tried," Srezzig replied. "Wasn't always enough."

"It was," Ukshagg said, her voice flat and unwavering.

Hashaezkend nodded. Shrarzeth flicked her tail in agreement. Drozkax stayed quiet, but the silence spoke loudly enough.

Shyvnir looked at them—the survivors, the rams, the thin gold light bleeding into the nest. Her mouth curved into something almost impossible: a smile. Small, but real. "Good," she said. "Now eat. Rest. The world will try to break you again tomorrow. Be ready."

The clutch dispersed—Ukshagg limping toward the crystal pools, Drozkax climbing to the high perch above the nest, Hashaezkend drifting toward the herd, and Shrarzeth settling herself along the rim to watch over the grazing rams.

Srezzig stayed.

Shyvnir called him with a quiet flick of her tail, her voice softer than he'd ever heard it. "You did well," she said. "You're what I hoped you'd be."

Srezzig swallowed, unsure where to place the weight of that. "Thank you," he managed—and meant it.

The matron's tail flicked again—gentle dismissal. Srezzig bowed his head and went to join the others.

For the first time in what felt like forever, the clutch felt whole.

They had learned how to make others run.

Night came down hard—sharp and cold as broken glass. Stars packed the sky so thick and bright they made the stone ridge glow.

Mother Shyvnir's voice rang out across the nest bowl, bouncing off the ancient walls as she called them in. Her claws clicked a steady beat while she paced the center, breathing blue-white heat into the old fire pit with every pass. Dust caught first, then flame—just a weak flicker at the start, swelling into a roaring column of bronze-blue fire that carved every shadow into stark relief.

They gathered around it, side by side, in the same formation they'd flown home.

Ukshagg's scales caught the firelight even through the scratches and dents. Shadows raced across her face with every flare, and she didn't blink once.

Hashaezkend sat at the far end, close enough that the blink rams had crept in behind her, as if they wanted to witness this too. Her eyes tracked everything, but her body was perfectly still—a stillness none of them had ever seen in her before.

Shrarzeth claimed the center spot, her newly healed leg planted solid beneath her. Her bronze hide drank in every drop of light and threw it back twice as bright.

Drozkax sprawled along one side, one leg extended as if in repose, but the posture didn't reach his shoulders, which stayed tight as he kept his head low. He was listening—really listening—harder than he'd ever listened to anything in his life.

Srezzig lingered at the edge. The lightning scar in his wing caught the starlight like it was answering back.

When the silence got heavy enough to feel, Shyvnir lifted her head.

"You came back," she said. Each word landed like a stone dropped from height. "You survived."

The pause stretched long and deliberate.

"But you're not the same clutch I sent out."

Nobody moved.

"You're something new," she continued, walking the circle slowly, deliberately. "Not just to me—to the world."

She stopped in front of Ukshagg first. The gold wyrmling's head jerked up like she expected a blow. Instead, Shyvnir uncurled her foreclaws. Resting there sat a shard of crystal—clear as frozen water, every edge splitting the firelight into impossible, dancing patterns.

"For seeing beyond sight," Shyvnir said. "For seeing what isn't there yet—and making it real."

Ukshagg took the crystal. Her expression shifted—pride, fear, hope, and something deeper beneath it—then she tucked the shard away like a secret meant only for her.

Hashaezkend was next. The matron offered a feather—long, white, its edges shimmering blue. "For feeling what others can't," she said softly. "For being brave enough to heal even when it costs you."

She placed it in Hashaezkend's palm. Hashaezkend stared at it for a long moment, eyes wet, then bowed her head in one sharp, grateful nod.

To Shrarzeth, Shyvnir gave a scale—her own, warm and curved, still humming faintly with old power. "For carrying the bloodline forward. For remembering where you came from."

Shrarzeth stared, stunned, then pressed the scale to her chest. It settled against her hide as if finding a missing piece, its faint glow a sign of acceptance into the bloodline.

For Drozkax, she drew out a stone—small, black, polished smooth. "From the river at the bottom of the world," she said. "Every weight tried to crush it. It remembers."

Drozkax turned the stone over in his claws, watching the firelight ripple across its surface. He looked up at the matron—just for a heartbeat—then closed his fist around it, jaw set.

Finally, Shyvnir turned to Srezzig. The entire nest held its breath.

She drew out a horn fragment, curved and sharp, the tip charred with a fused line of blue lightning running through it. "From a storm that killed a mountain," she murmured. "For the one who breaks but doesn't break. For the one who takes the hit—and turns it into a weapon."

She pressed it into his paw. Her grip was firm, almost grounding.

He took it. Heat bit straight through his scales. It felt like holding lightning, or the memory of every battle he'd ever survived.

The matron walked the circle once more, then settled by the fire. She didn't tell them she was proud. She didn't tell them they were ready. She simply said, "You're not wyrmlings anymore. You're dragons." Her voice dropped, quieter, almost reverent. "That is enough."

They sat in silence, each holding their gift, the air humming with possibility. The blink rams crept closer, drawn by the warmth and the strange quiet of the moment. Overhead, the stars wheeled across the sky—careless, brilliant, eternal.

The fire burned low, turning them all into silhouettes. Srezzig watched the others—Ukshagg tracing slow patterns in the dirt with her crystal, Hashaezkend spinning the feather between her claws, Shrarzeth clutching her scale like a medal, Drozkax staring into the embers with the river-stone clenched tight in his hand.

Nobody spoke. The silence said enough.

When the nest finally slept, Srezzig slipped away to the rim of the ridge. The cold bit hard, but the charge in his wing kept him warm. He climbed to the highest point—above the sleeping herd, above the fossil bones and ancient remains—and looked east, where the sky was starting to pale.

The world was still there. Broken, but open.

He stretched his wings—painful at first, then right—and let the wind catch the torn edge, tougher now than it had ever been.

He waited, letting the first light crawl up the cliffs, letting the electricity gather until he could taste the future sparking at the back of his tongue.

When the sun finally broke the horizon, Srezzig opened his wings wide, casting a shadow that stretched across the peaks, longer and darker than he ever imagined.

His wings could not yet span mountains.

The lightning in his veins, however, knew no such limits.

Afterword

This book began as a tie-in to *In the Company of Dragons* by Rite Publishing. Back in 2015, I was playing in a Pathfinder campaign run by Steve Russell, owner and publisher of Rite Publishing. I'd mentioned my interest in playing non-standard characters, and he introduced me to the *In the Company of...* series.

At the time, they were developing a new title, *In the Company of Dragons*, and Steve handed me a draft copy. I created a character using the early material and played through a full campaign with Steve as the Dungeon Master.

I was an aspiring writer then, and Steve freely shared his experience—offering advice on self-publishing, cover design, and the realities of the publishing world. When I told him I wanted to write a story about a group of young dragons—taninim, as they were named in the draft—he encouraged me to go for it.

In July 2016, Steve was killed in a car accident.

The story went onto a shelf and stayed there for years, untouched—until now.

Joab Stieglitz
November 2025

About The Author

Joab Stieglitz writes dark speculative fiction that blends dystopian worlds, moral ambiguity, and the quiet terror of systems that claim to protect humanity. His work explores power, identity, and survival under oppressive regimes, often through noir-inflected investigations and fractured societies on the brink of revolt. When he isn't writing, he builds immersive tabletop RPG worlds and studies the mechanics of control— both fictional and real. He lives in the United States.

You can follow Joab on Facebook, Bluesky, and on his blog: joabstieglitz.com.